THE WOMAN WHO LAUGHED

Also by Simon Mason

THE WOMAN WHO LAUGHED

Simon Mason

riverrun

First published in Great Britain in 2025 by

riverrun

An imprint of

Quercus Editions Limited
Carmelite House
50 Victoria Embankment
London EC4Y 0DZ

An Hachette UK company

The authorised representative in the EEA is Hachette Ireland,
8 Castlecourt Centre, Dublin 15, D15 XTP3, Ireland (email: info@hbgi.ie)

A CIP catalogue record for this book is available
from the British Library

Trade Paperback ISBN 978 1 52943 972 4
eBook ISBN 978 1 52943 973 1

1

Typeset in Plantin by CC Book Production
Printed and bound in Great Britain by Clays Ltd, Elcograf S.p.A.

Papers used by riverrun are from well-managed forests and other responsible sources.

For Eluned

In March 2020, as the coronavirus spread and the country prepared for lockdown, Ella Bailey, a sex worker in Sheffield, became Michael Godley's third victim. She was twenty-two years old. Godley had previously killed two other sex workers, one in Bradford, one in Wakefield, first bludgeoning them with a hammer then strangling them. All three were Black. In each city, Godley was known to prostitutes as an unusually brutal man, repeatedly terrorising and even injuring them, and, although Ella's body was never recovered, the police investigation collected more than enough evidence to conclude that Godley had killed and disposed of her. He was found guilty of all three murders and sentenced to a whole life term in prison, of which, it turned out, he served only a single year before being diagnosed with leukaemia. On his deathbed he made a full confession, describing how he had first bludgeoned then choked Ella Bailey to death with the strap of her own bag in an alley in the St Vincent's Quarter of Sheffield's inner city.

Five years later, the owner of a café in St Vincent's, arriving at half past seven to open up, found a lady's bag hanging neatly on his door handles. It was the bag Ella Bailey had been carrying when she was murdered; like her body, it had never been recovered. Coincidentally, later that morning, a vagrant being booked in the nearby Brocco Street police station casually mentioned that he'd seen Ella Bailey 'just now,' sitting on a bench in a local graveyard. The remark was treated with scepticism but the reappearance of the bag was not so easily explained. A day later, South Yorkshire police got in touch with me, and a day after that, on an August afternoon, I arrived in the city.

Around 170,000 people go missing in the UK every year. Within days almost all have returned or been found, though not always alive. Some – currently 5,000 or so – remain missing. They have escaped or been rescued. They have been captured, they have fled. Some have died, some have been killed. Others, perhaps, are simply lost, to themselves as much as to others. Many suffer from mental health problems, though not all. Some are presumed dead, who are not.

I'm a finder, a specialist, the result of my experiences, first in Paris, then London, where I developed certain skills, or perhaps sympathies, useful to the process of finding people. Perhaps it is mainly a question of temperament: most of the missing are found in the memories and imaginations of those who knew them. There, the reasons for their disappearance may first be detected, and it is simply by listening that the greater part of my work is done. In this way, I have been employed all over the country: police departments call me in for short, focused periods when they have a difficult or unusual case or their departmental budget is squeezed. Perhaps I am myself a sort of missing person, arriving and departing, appearing and disappearing. But, gradually, I have built up a reputation. I have become my work. My name is Talib but people call me 'Finder'.

Sheffield is a large and battered place, rising and falling across hills, sometimes a picturesque city, sometimes a threadbare one, crossed by rivers winding through pretty parks or channelled through aqueducts and culverts, the dirty brick remains of the heavy industry for which it is famous. In hot, bright weather I arrived at the rail station and took a taxi to the city centre to find my Airbnb, which was situated in a renovated historic building with a newly elegant foyer, gym and even cinema, now surrounded by clean new tower blocks, mostly for student accommodation but only a few hundred metres from desolate Upper Allen Street, where Ella had last been seen five years earlier. Stowing most of my things – I had brought with me only a small suitcase of clothes and toiletries and a copy of Jane Austen's *Persuasion* – I went out into the streets to get my bearings.

St Vincent's Quarter was once densely packed with factories, workshops and warehouses, the dark satanic mills of industry. Some of these remained, blackened and derelict, standing here and there in weed-choked lots, but whole blocks had been demolished and were now wastelands of rubble, out of which new buildings were slowly rising, smart student accommodation and smarter still luxury apartments for 'inner city living'. Many were still unfinished; as yet, they seemed like a few shiny parts of an unbuilt toy scattered across the broken-up ground. In general, the area was a startling mix of past and future, dead and living, lost and found.

For a while, I wandered through the streets, looking around. On brick walls were the faded painted signs of vanished metal-bashing occupations – *Stampers, Piercers* and *Metalworkers* – and the newer logos of current businesses squatting there now – *uPVC Windows and Doors*. Bulldozed streets were wide and glaring, others were narrow, steep and cobbled. From time to time I came across a corner store or fast food place. The people I encountered were notably friendly: the middle-aged man in a newsagent's where I stopped to buy a *Sheffield Star* addressed me several times as 'lovey' and, once, as 'ducky'.

After a while I became thirsty and stopped at a coffee shop on the corner of Edward Street and Scotland Street. Opposite was a massage parlour and, further down, a sauna; as I knew, at night the area was the red-light district. Brothels – like street prostitutes – are illegal in the UK, but they often operate in flimsy disguise as saunas and massage parlours, tolerated, at least for a while, by the authorities, and so assume a degree of respectability denied the young women who work the streets. I sat with a lemonade under an awning outside, thinking about these things and watching people go by. There weren't many: solitary students wearing backpacks, a few construction workers in hi-vis jackets. The area felt deserted, though I noticed more police officers than usual. There was a reason for this. The appearance of Ella's bag had coincided with the murder of another young woman. Like Ella Bailey, 'Sly' Stones had been a sex worker, soliciting on the surrounding streets, though her body had actually been found in the neighbouring university district, a quiet area of faculty buildings and plazas, peaceful and well-lit, where young students milled about with their coffees or sat relaxing in St George's Park at the end of Leavygreave Road; and the discovery of a body in the bushes there had given rise to a violent outcry against sex work, a campaign to 'clean up the city' and protect young people. Both the investigation into the unsolved murder and the passionate opinions about the issue filled the *Sheffield Star*, and the feeling on the streets of St Vincent's seemed both fearful and agitated.

I finished my lemonade and took a taxi out to police headquarters at Carbrook to meet my contact, DS Neeta Nunkoo.

DS Nunkoo briefed me in a meeting room on the fourth floor of the large smoked-glass building on the Carbrook Road, a cool, in fact antiseptic, place. We hadn't met before; she seemed very young, sleek and alert, her collar a little too tight, her eyes slightly bulging, but self-possessed and calm, with a habit of pausing for a moment between sentences, as if listening to an echo of herself. Although she hadn't been involved with the original investigation into Ella Bailey's murder, she'd taken the time to become familiar with its details.

She showed me two images. One was from an old newspaper cutting found inside the bag left hanging on the door handles a few days earlier. A frayed and softened scrap of print from an old *Sheffield Star*, it reported the triumph of fourteen-year-old Ella Bailey winning the 400-metre race at the national schools' championships, and the picture showed her crossing the finish line in full flow, strong and supple in victory, straining but smiling, almost laughing. It was a memento which Ella had carried with her always. The other photograph was a police image taken eight years later, just before she died. It showed a woman with a wasted face and weary, hate-filled expression, her lips chapped, her eyes sunk and leaking. Something – a twig, an insect, clotted dirt? – was clinging to her hair, giving her the appearance of a rough sleeper. If it wasn't for the pale birthmark on her forehead, it would be easy to assume the pictures were of two different people.

DS Nunkoo also showed me photographs of the bag, which was decorated with fringes and a distinctively bold black-and-white check pattern. It had, of course, been tested for fingerprints but, curiously, there were none.

Nunkoo summarised Ella's criminal record. By the age of twenty-two, she had been prosecuted twice for soliciting, three times for possession and, at the time of her death, had just been charged with the attempted armed robbery of a corner shop on Ecclesall Road. Although she had almost certainly been coerced into this by her boyfriend – a violent, feckless man called Caine Poynton-Smith – the evidence against her was very strong. She was looking at five to ten years, Nunkoo said. But, of course, the case against her was closed when she was murdered on that March night in 2020.

A week went by before anyone reported her missing, Nunkoo went on, and at first the investigation made little progress. Ella had last been seen on a Thursday night soliciting on the neighbourhood streets, and from the start it was feared that she was dead – the recent murders of the sex workers in Bradford and Wakefield were in everyone's minds – though, puzzlingly, no body was found, despite intensive, dog-assisted searches through streets with very few places in which to remain concealed. Then, after a delay, GPS tracking data was obtained from Ella's phone provider, which allowed the investigators to recreate her exact movements on the night of her disappearance.

At first, they were bewildered. For a few hours Ella had moved up and down the streets, evidently working her beat as usual. This went on until just before midnight, when she came to an abrupt stop at a point on Upper Allen Street next to a balti house. Now she no longer moved at all. Here, it seemed, she must have been killed. But at 6.00 a.m., after six hours' total inactivity, she'd unexpectedly set off again, this time going up and down the surrounding streets in a strange stop-start fashion, before making her way to Netherthorpe Road and hurrying north, just as her phone signal died.

The explanation for this strange behaviour was eventually provided by footage from a commercial CCTV camera outside a small paint supplies business in Upper Allen Street. It showed Ella at midnight standing at the entrance to a blind alley between the balti house and an abandoned brick shed. A man approaches and, after an exchange, disappears with Ella into the alley. Ten minutes later, disturbed by a passer-by, the man emerges from the alley and walks away up the street. Ella does not emerge, though there was no other way to exit the alley, which is blocked at the back with a high concrete wall. Nothing happens for six hours. Then an early-morning garbage truck appears. While it waits on the street, one of the refuse collectors goes into the alley to fetch the first of four wheelie bins, all of which are emptied in the usual way before the truck moves slowly on. Records subsequently acquired from the contractors showed that the movements of the truck – moving in stop-start fashion through the streets, then speeding away up Netherthorpe Road – exactly matched the last tracking data of Ella's phone. Moreover, the weight of the full load carried by the truck that morning was registered as above average – by about the weight of a human body. Together, the data seemed incontrovertible: Ella had been killed in the alley, dumped into one of the restaurant's wheelie bins and, a few hours later, unwittingly taken with the rest of the rubbish to one of the landfill sites that surround the city, where, after a delay of nearly two weeks, search teams had little chance of finding her.

Godley was arrested and in due course charged. Confronted with the CCTV evidence, he refused to accept it was him in the footage and denied being anywhere near Sheffield. Unfortunately for him, however, a speed camera had registered his car speeding at 12.20 a.m. that night less than a mile away. Furthermore, the passer-by who had disturbed him, whose name was Dean Burton, testified that the man who had emerged from the alley when he called out to him was indeed Michael Godley. At Godley's home in Wakefield the remains of clothing he was apparently wearing in the footage were found where he had tried to destroy them in a garden fire.

Case closed. Then, five years later, Ella's bag appeared. And a vagrant said he'd seen her sitting on a bench.

The vagrant's name was Flynn, though everyone called him Roof, because he'd once jumped off a local supermarket in the belief that he could fly and had broken both his legs. He was a notorious alcoholic who suffered delusions, and his statement about Ella Bailey had been prompted by overhearing two Brocco Street policemen talk about the discovery of Ella Bailey's bag while he waited for them to book him. DS Nunkoo, who clearly took most things seriously, did not attach any importance to what he'd said, though she suggested I talk to him myself.

The reappearance of the bag, however, was an indisputable fact, to which she had already devoted a lot of thought. It was certainly the same bag Ella is seen carrying when she went into the alley with Godley. Never found in the original investigation, it was thought to have ended up in the wheelie bin with Ella's body. Did its reappearance mean that she had somehow survived Godley's attack? Nunkoo did not believe it. She had a different theory: that it had been taken as a trophy by Ella's killer, who had chosen now to announce his reappearance. This was a radical thought. It would mean, among other things, that the original police investigation had got the wrong man, for the bag was never found among Godley's possessions; nor, of course, was he still around to hang it on the café door handles. Nunkoo rehearsed her argument. The CCTV footage was dark and not high quality; the man emerging from the alley has his beanie pulled down low over his forehead, making it impossible to identify him with one hundred per cent accuracy. His clothing is generic. Dean Burton's testimony was, of course, as fallible as any witness's. I pointed out that Godley had confessed, though I knew, as Nunkoo did, that confessions, like witness testimonies, are often unreliable. In his final days, Nunkoo said, Godley had been on heavy doses of morphine, he was emotional, his thoughts weren't clear; for instance, he had talked at length about episodes in his childhood that simply had not happened. Furthermore, she said, the bag found on the door handles had been carefully wiped of fingerprints: this was consistent with the idea of a trophy. If Ella had simply dropped it, obviously her fingerprints would be on it. She had yet another point to make, and showed me a photograph of a different ladies' bag hanging on a street sign at the edge of St George's Park. It belonged to Sly Stones, whose body had been found in bushes nearby. Sly's fingerprints were on it, but this bag too, the profilers said, could be considered as a trophy. Like Godley's other victims, and perhaps Ella as well, Sly had been both bludgeoned and choked. Taken together, Nunkoo said, the two bags might announce not so much the appearance of a new killer as the return of an old one.

I asked how the investigation into Sly's murder was progressing. Not well, Nunkoo told me. Information gathering was slow. It was thought that Sly had owed money to someone but they were still interviewing witnesses and reviewing available CCTV from all the obvious places – public spaces, private businesses, late-night buses, cashpoint machines (street prostitution is strictly a cash economy). Her fellow sex workers were, as usual, uncooperative.

I asked what they thought was going on.

They all thought, as she did, that Ella's actual killer had escaped justice five years earlier and had now returned to kill again, and, Nunkoo added, precisely because of their vulnerability, the girls' instincts were usually excellent. Of course, she added, they fought viciously among themselves, as was well known, but that too was a function of their circumstances. This led to her final point. Although my official brief was to explore the idea that Ella might still be alive – it was this, after all, that had unlocked the budget to hire me – I should, from the beginning, consider the possibility that the girls on the street were right, that Ella had been murdered five years earlier – just not by Godley.

The briefing was over. She provided me with all the log-in details and access codes that I would need and asked me if I had any questions. I said only one. How many hours of CCTV of the alley entrance had the investigators reviewed? A full twenty-four hours, she said, from 11.00 p.m. on the night of Ella's disappearance to 11.00 p.m. the following night, although now, she added, it existed only in the form presented at the trial, a nine-hour section from 11.00 p.m. to 8.00 a.m.

She looked at her watch. She had arranged for Flynn to be available for interview at the Brocco Street station, and said that she would drive me there herself.

Brocco Street station, just round the corner from my Airbnb, was little more than a front desk and a few offices, one of which was used for interviews. It was here that Nunkoo and I met Flynn, a wild-looking Black man with overgrown hair and beard nearly entirely grey and a wide, chaotic smile. He had been a fixture in St Vincent's for twenty years, a well-known sight, shuffling along the streets, fishing in bins or sleeping on benches. Like many homeless, he struggled with addiction and mental health issues and though he often spent nights in a local refuge, he had never managed to pass any of the eligibility tests to qualify for more permanent housing. Incredibly, he remained cheerful.

I'd read the transcript of his statement, in which he said he'd come across Ella sitting on a bench in the graveyard of St George's Church at about 10.00 a.m. two days earlier as he walked through the park towards Mappin Street. He described her as looking very well. She'd recognised him, he said, and greeted him as he passed by, but he didn't stop because he'd been busy at just that moment; and when he looked back a few moments later she'd gone.

Nunkoo explained to Flynn that I wanted to ask him a few questions about this, and he nodded and gestured affably, though as soon as I started to talk he interrupted to say that he was busy and would have to leave very soon. I said I wouldn't keep him long, and he found that funny.

I asked him how well he knew Ella Bailey. They were friends, he told me. I asked if he'd been surprised to see her again after so long and he shook his head. People, he said, and grinned, showing gaps. He had more he wanted to say about people but I went on with my questions and he listened attentively. In his statement he'd said that Ella had looked well. What did he mean? Good, he said, she'd looked good. Happy, he added. All her troubles had gone away, he added. I asked him what he thought she'd been doing on the bench. He had no idea. Did she look as if she were waiting for someone? He hadn't thought of that. What had she been wearing? The 'usual', he said. Nunkoo reminded him that he'd mentioned a short skirt and some sort of flimsy top, and he frowned. It was hard to remember, he'd never been much interested in clothes. He himself was wearing a soiled army jacket and torn grey sweatpants. A hat, he said suddenly. A big hat. Nunkoo pointed out that he hadn't mentioned a hat before. I asked him what colour and he said with suspicious promptness, 'Pink,' and grinned. He was enjoying himself. I asked if he'd spoken to Ella. No, he hadn't, but she'd spoken to him, he said. She greeted him, very friendly. 'Hey, Walt.' He nodded, remembering. They'd always been good friends. He didn't say anything in reply, it was too early for talk, he said, but he'd nodded back and smiled and wiggled his fingers, and she'd sort of laughed. After he'd walked past her, he thought of something to say, which he couldn't now remember, and he'd turned back, but she'd gone, so he'd just waved at the empty bench and gone on. He'd been busy, he said again.

Nunkoo said, 'Your name isn't Walt.'

He became perturbed.

I asked if Ella had had her bag with her, and he brightened again. Yes, he told me, that was the thing he remembered best. She had it on her lap, a black-and-white bag with fringes. He described the bag in great detail.

We thanked him then and left him, and went out together to the lobby. Nunkoo pointed out the obvious: that Flynn could not have seen Ella with her bag at ten in the morning when the café owner had already handed it in to the police.

Clearly, she said, Flynn had heard the policemen talking about it at the station. It seemed likely. I asked Nunkoo if she thought it was curious that Flynn should think he saw Ella in St George's Park, where Sly's body had recently been found, and she replied that because the park had been in the news a lot it wasn't surprising that someone like Flynn should associate it with another murdered prostitute. This was also true. Besides, she added, St George's Park was where Flynn was generally to be found. Everything she said made sense, and I thanked her and, leaving her there, went out of the air-conditioned chill of the station into the heat of the day, fierce now, and flagged down a taxi to take me to see Ella's foster-parents.

Knowle Lane was a tree-shady road of trim green verges and impeccable hedges in middle-class Ecclesall, and the house where Ted and Mary Bailey still lived – where Ella had grown up – was a solid semi-detached villa with imposing bay windows behind a front garden laid out with stone ornaments around a tiny circular pond containing two silver carp, which rose obligingly to the surface as I arrived. The Baileys were in their early sixties, both white, Ted a little hunched with hollowed face, thick-rimmed glasses and big, unsteady hands which he made efforts to keep in his lap, Mary slight and softened in a pale yellow summer dress and sensible shoes. They had already identified the newspaper cutting in the bag as Ella's, but, telephoning ahead, I'd asked them if they might show me some more photographs of their foster-daughter, and now Mary laid a selection before me in the front room where we sat. She had fetched them from a trunk upstairs, she said with a glance at Ted, they didn't keep photos of their adopted daughter on display. Ted's expression slid away from her stonily.

All the photos showed a happy child, swooping towards the camera on a swing, riding a bicycle, sitting cross-legged with a book on a lawn. There were no photos of her older than fourteen. Mary, following my eyes as I turned from one to another, told me that Ella had been easy to please when she was small. She was popular at her junior school, a girl who enjoyed life, who liked to laugh. Physical, out-doorsy, a bit of a dare-devil: she used to say that when she grew up she wanted to be a stunt performer in the movies. But she was clever, too, a clever little girl. And of course determined. That came out later, in her athletics. For a while Mary reminisced about family holidays at Tudweiliog in Wales, Coverack in Cornwall. It was only later, she said after a pause, that there had been problems. Ted spoke. 'Drugs,' he said, and looked away through the window. Mary frowned. 'Much later,' she said. But it was true that once Ella had reached puberty, she became more dissatis-fied, more headstrong. She had always been bold, always the first to meet a challenge, but now she became confrontational. It was hard to say why. From the beginning she'd known that she was fostered – obviously there was no hiding it – but, as she grew older, she seemed to find it increasingly difficult to accept. They agreed to support her in finding her biological mother, but her mother turned out to be having difficulties of her own – she was living in a hostel for recovering alcoholics – and refused to see Ella. After that, Ella started to devote herself to athletics, but she also became distrustful, prickly, as if she constantly felt people were disrespecting her. Those were difficult years, Mary said. Her teachers complained about Ella's attitude. She was accused of stealing some sports equipment from the school gym and though the sports master later withdrew the accusation, the damage was done: Ella took it as a sign that no one trusted her. Finally, Mary said, there was a serious incident at school and she was asked to leave. 'Expelled,' Ted said, his hands moving restlessly in front of him. 'Expelled then,' Mary said. At any event, she moved to a new school where she never seemed to fit in or get on. Her new sports master seemed to regard her as a liability; she wouldn't work with him and soon dropped her athletics altogether. She didn't have any real friends anymore, only other disaffected pupils, most of them older than her. And then, when she was sixteen, she met Caine.

Again Mary glanced at Ted, who was gripping his hands tightly together now. Caine was six years older than Ella, Mary said, twenty-two when they met, and from the beginning the relationship was inappropriate. Not that either Mary or Ted ever properly met him; they would see him hanging about in the lane with his hood concealing his face or a woollen hat pulled down low, waiting for Ella to come out. At first he had a motorbike, then a derelict Toyota, then a Range Rover with blacked-out windows. Ella wouldn't talk about Caine to them because, she said, they were prejudiced. Once, Ted went out to confront him, but the young man just sneered at him. Ella began to stay out late, played truant from school. There were bitter arguments. When she was seventeen they found drugs in her room and when they tried to talk to her about them she reacted with fury. 'Not respecting her privacy,' Ted said from his chair, angrily addressing the far wall. 'The usual *claptrap*.' He was becoming angry. Mary sat quietly, as if trying to dissolve the memory. 'Perhaps we were too harsh with her,' she said at last. But, she went on, anyone who had experienced problems with teenagers, especially if there are drugs involved, would recognise the anguish of parents and the sheer difficulty, perhaps impossibility, of arriving at conclusions satisfactory to everyone. So their arguments continued, and when Ella was eighteen there was a decisive row and she left home. Ted spoke, this time at length but again addressing the wall. Ella claimed he kicked her out, he said, but he hadn't, he wanted me to know that, *she* left *them*; she told them she never wanted to see them again and after that the only time they spoke to her was at the police station. Many times they went looking for her, at Jordanthorpe, where she was living with Caine, or in St Vincent's, where they discovered she was 'spending time'. They liaised with the police, with various departments of the social services, but because Ella was over eighteen by then, they had no influence and Ella refused to cooperate with any of the professionals who reached out to her. 'We lost her,' Ted said in a furious and desperate voice. 'We lost her,' Mary repeated quietly after a moment.

I asked them questions about the bag and what they thought its reappearance might mean. Ted did not believe it meant Ella was still alive. On the contrary, he thought – like DS Nunkoo – that the police had wrongly convicted Godley, and the unknown man who had actually killed Ella had kept the bag all this time as a sick memento, displaying it now when he'd committed a second murder. It was his view, he went on, that there was a sickness in society. Mary tried to interrupt but he spoke over her, hands jumping in his lap. A depravity, he said, caused by narcotic drugs, the

25

selling of them, the consuming of them. There were drugs even in Ecclesall, he'd seen dealers selling them openly in the street, addicts taking drugs in the nearby parks, he'd come across their needles and bags and other paraphernalia in the gutters of the neighbouring leafy lanes. And where there were drugs, he said, there was crime, muggings, corner shops robbed, houses burgled, their own house for instance, here in middle-class Ecclesall, broken into just the other day by some out-of-control person, even their allotment had been vandalised, and who would vandalise an allotment, he asked furiously, *addicts*, that's who, he said, answering himself, addicts looking for a quiet place to inject themselves. Though he was gasping for breath by now, he went on, more loudly still. That piece of *filth* – meaning Caine Poynton-Smith – had corrupted Ella, poisoned her with drugs, pimped her. Here Mary again tried to interject, but still he ignored her, his voice rising further. Yes he did, he said, they knew well enough what work she'd been doing, and that man – meaning Caine – *pimped* her to earn money to fund his own addiction, he forced her to take a knife into that corner store to steal money to pay for his drugs and his deals, and she *gave herself to him*, he said, groaning, she left us, she said we never loved her, he went on fiercely, panting now, but we did, *we did*, he shouted, glaring at me now as if challenging

26

me to defy him. After this there was a silence. 'We did love her,' Mary said quietly after a moment.

As I waited to let the emotion settle, Mary asked me if I had children of my own and, caught up in their drama, I nearly said yes but stopped myself in time and asked her instead what she made of the reappearance of Ella's bag. Did she agree with Ted? Speaking without looking at her husband, she didn't answer the question but said that Ella had always been such a spirited girl that she felt that something of that spirit must have remained in her. She had always felt, in fact, that one day Ella would have found the strength to come to her senses and rid herself of her addiction and leave her boyfriend and begin to lead a normal life again.

I asked them what Ella might do now if she were alive and had come back to Sheffield. Would she come here?

'No,' Ted said at once. She would go straight back to him, that piece of filth.

There was a silence in the room which seemed terminal and I got up to leave. Mary came with me, and on the doorstep, with the pretty front garden glowing in the late afternoon sun, we stood for a moment together. She apologised for her husband's outburst: the recent break-ins had upset him, she said. I said that I had a final question for her. What was the incident at school that had led to

Ella's expulsion? Mary said that Ella had attacked a boy, breaking his cheekbone in two places and hospitalising him. The reason for her attack was never explained: he was two years older than Ella and there had been no prior contact between them. Ella simply refused to comment. There must have been a reason, Mary said, the boy might have made some derogatory comment, about Ella being fostered or even about her being Black, though if that were true, obviously the matter should have been reported so the school could deal with it. But by then Ella distrusted her teachers and, to be frank, Mary said, she was prone to bouts of uncontrolled anger, unable to control her emotions. She frequently clashed with Ted at that time. He'd been a strict father, insisting on good behaviour, doing the right thing, thinking of others before yourself, paying your debts. His own father had been an evangelical preacher. But perhaps he was too insistent, she said, too harsh. 'Anyway,' she went on, 'somewhere in her childhood we lost her, we failed her. She said that we didn't care about her because she was fostered, but the truth,' Mary said, 'was that she was precious to us always.' She remembered her as a child, laughing. She wished that was all she could remember.

She hesitated then, and I saw she had something else she wanted to tell me. She lowered her voice and told me she had seen Ella a few days before her disappearance. Ted did not know this. In those final years Ted always refused to see Ella, he'd turned away from her completely, wouldn't even talk to Mary about her, though it pained him terribly because his feelings for her were as strong as any father's, as I'd undoubtedly seen for myself. Anyway, without telling him, Mary would occasionally slip out to meet Ella somewhere in town. She was often in need of money, Mary said apologetically, though it was obvious to her that Ella would spend it on drugs. That last time they'd met, in a café in Atkinsons department store in town, Ella was emaciated, on edge, even a little paranoid, continually scratching her thin arms, looking round wildly as if expecting to see someone who wasn't there. She kept saying that she'd had enough. It was then, Mary said, that she felt sure Ella was going to leave Caine. Since the attempted robbery of the corner shop, she was terrified of going to prison. She'd hit rock bottom, Mary said, she could no longer live as she had been doing and she knew that escaping from her controlling boyfriend was necessary.

I asked her if Ella had actually told her about leaving Caine and she hesitated. She couldn't remember Ella's exact words but she'd seen it in her face. It was plain to her, she said, she was Ella's mother after all. Foster-mother, she corrected herself, but it amounted to the same thing, she'd brought Ella up from a baby, she had the same feelings for her child as any natural mother would. She had begun quietly to cry and I thanked her for her courage, and found, as we stood there in silence, that I had one more thing to ask her, the question which she hadn't answered before. Did she believe Ella was still alive? She flinched, and I saw by her expression that she did not. Yes, she lied, yes I do, she said, and out of sheer bravery held my eyes a moment, her face wet but calm, before turning and going back into the house, leaving me in the sunlit garden with the carp rising and sinking in the little pond.

Back at my Airbnb, I unpacked, then went out to walk round St Vincent's again, thinking over my conversation with Ella's foster-parents. Ella had been a child who loved to laugh, Mary had told me. The comment found a strange echo in Flynn's fantasy that the adult Ella had laughed when he wiggled his fingers at her in St George's Park.

After such a hot day, the air was thick and greasy, and after a few hours I became thirsty. As the light failed, I stopped at a cheap café in an out-of-the-way street and drank Chinese tea and ate noodles and read my copy of *Persuasion*. I had picked out the book at the last minute and now it seemed a strange, even disconcerting, choice. The curious coincidence that Austen's heroine, Anne Elliot, was the same age in the book – twenty-seven – as

Ella Bailey would be if she were still alive, struck me. But, in general, St Vincent's razed streets formed a stark contrast with the elegant houses of Austen's Elliots and Musgroves, a dream world that could no longer exist. When it grew dark I left the restaurant and went to take a closer look at the alley where Ella had – or hadn't – been killed.

Upper Allen Street was poorly lit. At the far end I could see new student accommodation blocks; at the end where I stood were leftover brick sheds covered in graffiti, waste ground filled with scrub, everything obscured by shadows, a place battered by long years of industrial decline. The balti house had closed down, the building that remained was a shell, metal grilles covering its windows and door, matching the ruined brick shed on the other side of the alley. Perhaps, once, this 'alley' had provided access to the land behind the buildings, but it had long ago been closed off. Now it extended only a few metres into the darkness before ending in a high concrete wall topped with broken glass and barbed wire. There was absolutely no way out except via the entrance. Weeds were growing thickly along its margins and towards the rear the ground was strewn with rubbish and piles of lumber. It looked very like it did in the footage of five years earlier: all that was missing were the wheelie bins. Walking into it, I smelled the stink of animal excrement and, looking up at the high walls surrounding me, tried to imagine Ella escaping after being attacked. It did not seem possible, yet I already knew that in her youth Ella had been someone who did unusual things, thinking not only of her athletic achievements but of the 'uncontrollable' temper mentioned by her foster-mother, her unprovoked attack on a boy at school and, even more striking, her refusal to justify or even explain it.

It was midnight and I made my way back to my Airbnb. It was still warm. On Scotland Street, two young women stood close together, another talked to a man in a car. Despite their fear of a killer on the loose, they were still working. The foyer of my building was naturally deserted at that time but as I climbed the grand stairway and went along the hallway, it seemed the whole place was dead, the apartments largely unoccupied. They would have been too expensive for students and perhaps demand for the luxurious inner city living which the building's owner advertised had not yet materialised. However, as I unlocked the door to my apartment, I heard faint music coming from the apartment opposite and at that moment its door opened, a young woman appeared and stood there looking at me.

'Hey,' she said after a moment, as if amused by finding me in front of her.

I asked her if she had been expecting someone else, and she continued to scrutinise me.

No, she said at last. She made it a rule not to expect anything, she added. Expectation was the enemy of possibility.

All the time, she continued to look at me intently. She was very young, perhaps only eighteen or nineteen years old, short and spare, wearing a slogan T-shirt, baggy calf-length cargo trousers and basketball boots. Her hair was cropped and dyed peroxide blonde, and she had the sort of bodily looseness I associate with those who do yoga and the very self-assured. The slogan on her T-shirt said *Ceci n'est pas un T-shirt* and she stood there as if waiting for me to do something. I explained that I was staying in the apartment just for a few days on business and she continued to look at me. She seemed amused. After a moment she asked me what I thought of Jane Austen. She had noticed my copy of *Persuasion*. I said that I liked her books and asked her what she thought. 'I'll give her five for style,' she said at last. I asked if she meant Austen's literary style, and she said no, she meant her descriptions of clothing and furnishings. 'And a bonus point for the stuff about the marriage market.' I asked her if she was a student of literature and again she paused a long time before replying. 'Fine Arts,' she said at last. 'Call them arts, call them fine.' I laughed then, remembering being a student myself, how keen I'd been to make an impression, to avoid the

inconsequential in conversations, to make striking pro-
nouncements, feeling that such things were not at all showy
or trivial, as other people must have found them, but
important parts of the most exciting thing of all, the inven-
tion of my teenage self; and I thought that this young
woman was engaged in precisely this enterprise now. I
observed that it was a nice upmarket place for a student to
live but before she could reply, if indeed she had been going
to, she seemed to hear something in her apartment, a
change of music perhaps or someone moving about, and
prepared to go. I told her my name and she nodded without
comment. 'You can call me Puck,' she said after a moment,
then retreated into her apartment and shut the door.

My own apartment had the well-appointed features and
neat finish of hotel rooms, the sort of unlived-in imperson-
ality that always makes me feel that I've entered a
photograph. All traces of it ever having been occupied had
been removed. It felt empty, even with me in it. In the
showroom-like kitchen I drank a glass of water, then settled
myself in the living room with my laptop and ran the CCTV
footage to which DS Nunkoo had given me access.

As I'd seen already, the alley hadn't changed much in
the intervening years. At midnight on that Thursday in
March 2020 it had been dark, of course, but the filthy

concrete ground and piles of rubbish among the weeds were visible as far back as the first of the wheelie bins. Beyond was total darkness. The balti house to the left of the alley had closed for the night; the other building, to the right of it, was already a ruin.

Ella Bailey stands at the entrance wearing a thin jacket, short skirt, boots. Her features are hard to make out, but she holds the distinctive bag found five years later. Something off camera attracts her attention and she adopts a pose, part showy, part insolent. A moment later the man identified as Godley comes into sight and stops in front of the balti house. He is wearing a thick, shapeless jacket and a beanie pulled low over his forehead; his face is never fully visible. The body language of both of them is awkward: she is flighty, dithering on her high-heeled boots; he seems fixed into position. They talk, almost seem to argue. He keeps his distance so she has to lean forward to hear him. After this exchange she turns to look into the alley. Then he steps forward and takes hold of her by the shoulder and walks with her into the shadows, she moving a little unsteadily, her jacket in her hand, her bag over her shoulder, he a little behind her, walking stiffly, almost as if in pain, seeming to close in on her urgently as they disappear beyond the bins into darkness. For several minutes nothing happens, the footage runs without change, the scene is empty and still. Then another figure appears in front of the balti house, a man smaller and slighter than Godley, wearing an overcoat and flat cap, walking slowly, drifting past the alley entrance as if out walking his dog, though no dog appears, before stopping suddenly to peer into the shadows, cocking his head as if to catch something he has heard. This is Dean Burton. He appears to call out, still nothing happens, then just when he is about to move off again, Godley appears out of the shadows. At first, in the darkness, he is just a vague impression of movement, then he appears fully, walking slightly hunched past Dean to exit the alley, turning back up the street and disappearing off camera. Dean gazes after him for a moment, looks again into the alley, then continues down the street in the opposite direction.

The original investigators thought that the man – Godley or not – walked in that hunched fashion because he was concealing a hammer under his jacket. Nunkoo now thought it was Ella's bag he was hiding. Either was possible.

I watched this section of footage several times and saw nothing more in it. There was nothing to see in the next few hours either, which I speeded through: no passers-by, no traffic, not even an urban fox or rat. Slight changes in the weather, a changing tilt in the angle of the shadows: nothing else. Then, at six o'clock in the morning, when it was still as dark as ever, a garbage truck pulls up. A man jumps out of the cab and disappears into the alley, soon reappearing at the back of the truck hauling two wheelie bins. He pushes them into position to be lifted and emptied in the usual way, then drags them back into the alley, reappearing a few moments later to repeat the process with two more bins, after which he rejoins the driver in the cab, and the truck moves off again down the street. Though I watched this process several times, there was nothing in the man's movements to suggest anything unusual. In the statement he made to the police at the time, he commented that when he'd arrived one of the bins was on its side, which was taken by the prosecution as the sign of a possible struggle, though the man specifically said bins were often found like that. More suggestively, he said that one of the bins was particularly heavy. What interested me, however, was the position of the truck. For the few minutes it waited there, it obscured the camera view of the alley.

By the time I went to bed it was late, but for a little while I read *Persuasion* before settling down to sleep. In my sleepy mind were Puck's comments about clothing and furnishings, which I did not find persuasive, and the marriage market, which I did. As is well known, Anne Elliot, our unmarried heroine, has failed in this market, persuaded against her instincts some years earlier to break off her engagement with the young seaman Frederick Wentworth. For different reasons, her elder sister Elizabeth has also failed, marriage-wise. The family is 'distressed' for want of money, so these failures are serious. And in due course, other single women – the vivacious Musgrove cousins – will enter the market, providing new competition. Austen gives us a group of smiling, polite women who are rivals, playing by certain established rules, well or badly. Social laws, human nature, temperament and circumstances, these are the basic elements of the story. I remembered DS Nunkoo's comments that the young women who worked the streets fought viciously among themselves, and I thought again of fourteen-year-old Ella's unprovoked attack on a boy for reasons she refused to explain. The rules by which we play are not always straightforward. And finally I settled down to sleep, hearing in the still darkness of the building faint music from Puck's apartment across the hall.

It was just as hot the next day. When I drew back the curtains, the street was already a sheer white glare in the sun, and, as I sat in the foyer waiting for my taxi, I reflected that for many it would be a day of discomfort, for the English are not used to such relentless temperatures and it does not take much heat before they are irritably longing for their drizzle. It doesn't bother me, born and brought up in Baghdad, where the heat is so much greater and lasts much longer, but after so many years in the north even I feel the inappropriateness of the English heatwave, the sun beating down on those grey, hunched houses built for rain.

It had been a wet night five years earlier when Ella Bailey burst into a little store on Ecclesall Road and held a knife to the shopkeeper's face. In his testimony, he said that she appeared to be out of control, no doubt high, hands shaking, eyes unfocused, and he was frightened she might hurt him by mistake, even as he was opening the till to give her the money she demanded. As it happened, she never got it. At that moment a group of young men came into the store together and, after a ghastly hesitation in which, the shopkeeper said, anything might have happened, Ella turned and ran out. She was arrested the following day but released after an intervention by her appointed solicitor, and the investigation was still ongoing when she disappeared. The police team had no doubts about what she had done but there were problems collecting sufficient evidence. No in-store CCTV existed and the video taken by one of the young men was inadmissible: it existed only as a copy on someone else's phone and, as such, had been rejected by the prosecution services. Statements from Ella's foster-parents, which I had read, gave the view that Ella had been coerced into the attempted robbery by her boyfriend, and this was supported by Ella's addiction counsellor. Perhaps Caine Poynton-Smith would have joined Ella on trial if the case hadn't been dropped. Previously, and subsequently, he'd been arrested a number of times, in some cases on suspicion of possession, once for assault, though never charged. Today he was still living in Jordanthorpe, in a maisonette in Ormond Close, not far from the A61, and that's where I asked my taxi to take me.

The idea that Ella might return to Caine rather than to Ted and Mary interested me, less because of her possible feelings for him, and more because they made it seem that her break with them was permanently irrevocable. She was not an apologiser or reconciler.

I'd seen a photograph of Caine aged twenty-two, shortly after he met Ella, a good-looking skinny white boy with inked arms and floppy dark hair in vest and fedora hat. His expression was playful, calculating and self-satisfied all at once. Ten years later he wore exactly the same outfit, though his hair had receded, his vest was tight around the middle and his expression as I introduced myself was wary bordering on insolent. He did not want to talk about Ella Bailey, did not want to talk to me at all, did not want me in his house, wanted me, in fact, to fuck off, but he wasn't a man who could sustain any sort of attitude for long and once I showed him my police credentials he reluctantly let me in. His living room was crowded with electronic equipment, cables and packing crates, and he sprawled on a couch, sneering at the wall and pretending I wasn't there. I knew from his biography in police files that he was a man of pretences. He had grown up in Bolton but ran away to Sheffield when he was seventeen and hung around clubs

and music studios pretending he knew about sound engin-
eering until he was hired by a small outfit based in Firth
Park, north of the city centre. He liked to pretend to girls
that he was a musician himself, a 'creative'. Also, that he
would be nice to them. In fact, over the years, he'd been
questioned more than once about violent outbursts against
women and had only escaped charges of assault against a
former girlfriend and mother of his child because the police
failed to present evidence in the correct manner. He was
currently attempting to regain visiting rights but he kept
getting into trouble. He didn't seem like someone who
habitually used violence, but rather someone who might
lose control. He did not seem intelligent.

I asked him if he'd seen Ella recently and he turned to
me, a confused, perhaps fearful, expression on his face,
which he covered at last with a sneer. She's dead, he said.
She's been dead years. He quickly looked away, once more
attempting an air of jaded indifference.

I asked then if this was where he'd been living with Ella
five years earlier and he acknowledged it. Lighting a cigarette, he ignored me but I could see that the urge to
justify himself was strong in him. She was a nightmare, he
said at last. People didn't realise, didn't understand, they
said he'd been a bad influence on her. A joke, he said, a
fucking joke, it was exactly the other way round, she was

a bad influence on him. Ella got him into drugs. She'd been using when he met her and she was only sixteen. *Sixteen,* he said. He looked at me as if to gauge the effect of what he was saying. She could be violent too, he added, thinking perhaps he wasn't making his point forcefully enough. Once, near the end, she went after him with a hot iron. Thing is, he said, she grew up posh but she was bad. He flicked ash on to the carpet. Fucking nightmare, he said again and shrugged, a bitter, dismissive gesture intended to convey helplessness in the face of her appalling behaviour.

I said that it sounded like a volatile situation and asked if Ella had been planning to move out in the weeks before her disappearance.

Once more he hesitated. Chance would be a fine thing, he said after a moment.

I asked him why he'd waited a week before reporting her missing and he shrugged. She'd often stayed away for days on a rampage, he said, but she always came back in the end. He'd come close once or twice to dumping her stuff in the road while she was away but despite everything he'd still had feelings for her, even at the end. I waited, and in a little while he went on. She was good-looking, he said, apart from that blot on her forehead, and to be fair, she'd been exciting to be with, he'd give her that, at least at first;

she could make people laugh, she had a nice laugh, he said, until she began to lose her teeth, but she couldn't control herself, that was the point, she'd do anything for drugs, even go on the street and give blow-jobs to old men, though he'd begged her not to, many times he'd tried to persuade her to stop, though there was never any stopping Ella, he said. It tore him up to see her on the street. A woman couldn't go any lower than whoring. He never had anything to do with them.

I pointed out that he'd been questioned a few months earlier by the police about pimping sex workers.

Again a hesitation. Usual police-type bullshit, he said. Desperate stuff, pathetic. He busied himself lighting another cigarette. She was a junkie whore, he said; if he'd never met her he never would have tried drugs himself. He sat there, affecting indifference.

I pointed out that in the five years since Ella's death, far from taking the opportunity to clean himself up, he'd continued to use; twice in the last year he'd been questioned not only about suspected possession but also dealing. According to some, he'd been seen round St Vincent's with a 'bag of goodies'. Also, I said, down in the university campus area by St George's Park, where Sly Stones was killed.

His leg began to twitch. He denied it. I was missing his

point. Without Ella provoking him into reckless behaviour, he'd developed a much more relaxed attitude to what he referred to as 'recreationals'. With her, he said, everything had been chaotic, drugs-wise, she'd been getting into fights, robbing. Alone, he was a different person, relaxed, calm, more like himself. He wasn't the kind of person to lose his cool.

But even as he said it, I could see how irritable he was becoming. I mentioned the attempted armed robbery on Ecclesall Road. There was circumstantial evidence that he had coerced Ella. Still more bullshit, he said. He snatched the cigarette out of his mouth and jabbed it at me. Ella was the violent one, he'd told me that already, she'd always been violent, was known for it, even when she was young, she'd been expelled from school for hospitalising some kid. He'd only ever defended himself. And she got worse after she went on the street, he added, girls there were feral, scratched each other's eyes out if you trespassed on their beat, she'd come home at dawn, black eye, blood on her face. Chaos, he said. Chaos is what it was.

He finished his cigarette and, as if that were a cue, nodded towards the door, but I stayed where I was, looking round the cluttered room. The anonymity of it struck me, there was nothing personal in it, no photographs on display, no objects expressive of personality. I asked if he'd kept any of Ella's things as keepsakes, and he frowned at me suspiciously and glanced away. A photo, I suggested, jewellery, an item of clothing. A bag? He denied it, though, oddly, his eyes went round the room, as if anxiously checking nothing was there. He'd got rid of it all five years ago, he said, he didn't want to be reminded of her. I pursued the theme, asking him about the newspaper cutting which had been found in the bag left on the café door handles and which Ella's foster-parents said was hers. He scoffed at that. In all the time they were together he'd never once seen this famous newspaper cutting, it was his opinion that her foster-parents were making a drama out of it to cover up the fact that they'd had such a shit relationship with her. They'll tell you they loved her, he said, warming to his theme, but they were the worst, the absolute fucking worst. The old man used to run out of the house and try to chase him away, he'd even seized hold of him once and Caine had been forced to defend himself. Several times he'd seen him get hold of Ella in the same way, he added. If I was at all interested in violence, he said, I should think a bit about that, instead of making up stuff about him. Foster-parents don't care the same way, he added.

He was lighting another cigarette, hands trembling, and barely glanced at me as I got up to leave. From the door, I looked back at him sitting hunched on the couch, flicking ash on the soiled carpet, his arms slack, face already pouched, his whole heroin chic – hat, vest, tattoos – looking battered and worn and on edge. His youth had gone sour. He seemed like a person engulfed by bad habits.

Looking up, he expressed surprise that I hadn't left yet.

I said I had one more question for him but it wasn't about Ella. Where had he been on the night Sly Stones was murdered? Now all his pretended indifference fell away; I'd pushed him too far. He got to his feet fast, eyes bulging, and came up to me at the door, and as we faced each other I had to remind him that if he did anything stupid he would certainly not regain the right to see his child. He seemed about to lose control but after a moment he pulled himself away, sneering, and simply told me to get the fuck out of his house; and I left, going out into the hot sunshine, a white glare on the tarmac of the road.

I was already a little late for my next meeting. In the taxi I called DS Nunkoo and asked her if Caine Poynton-Smith had been questioned in connection with the Sly Stones murder. She said that in fact he had; he had money-related connections with Sly, but that evening he'd been in Birmingham managing the sound for a gig. She asked me in turn what my thoughts about him were. In truth, I'd found him unconvincing, though I did not yet know if this was related to something specific or his character in general. To Nunkoo I mentioned only the comments made by Ella's foster-father, that if Ella were alive and had returned to Sheffield she would go not to her foster-family but to her former boyfriend, and she wasn't very interested in that but to please me said that she would organise a review of relevant surveillance footage from the last few days around the Jordanthorpe area. Then my taxi pulled up outside Whirlowdale Secondary School, and I paid the driver and went in to meet Ms Bell, who had been Ella's teacher a dozen years earlier.

The school sat at the edge of woodland, where the road ran out of the trees towards the open countryside of Derbyshire. The whole suburb was conspicuously affluent, with large semi-detached houses and wide grass verges, and the school itself gave the appearance of both confidence and expectation, motivational slogans everywhere, artworks by students in Reception which would not have looked out of place in a gallery, and posters along the corridors showing joyously expressive children in a variety of stimulating situations. As I waited there, listening to high-spirited noises from the playgrounds outside, I thought of my own school in Baghdad, plainer and older, though in fact even more exclusive, a quiet place removed from the general life of the city, to which my father brought me each day in his car. There, it seemed to me now, I had no thought of anything except myself, a boy among other boys, with little understanding of what I was doing, barely aware of the nature of the school and what it meant to be there, and of course no inkling of what was to come afterwards: Operation Desert Storm, Paris, my uncle's apartment, London, my wife and son, my future. A bell went, the voices outside drained away, and I wondered what future the young Ella Bailey had dreamed about when she was one of the pupils here at Whirlowdale school.

Ms Bell came to greet me herself and we went together to the senior management suite, where she had her office. Years earlier she'd been Ella's History teacher; now she was Deputy Head, a middle-aged lady with auburn hair, elegant in carnation-pink trouser suit and floral scarf. Her accent was Home Counties, though she said she'd lived in Sheffield for twenty-five years and would never leave.

'Its reputation for friendliness is entirely deserved,' she said as she poured coffee. Her smile was warm but brief as she moved on to address the reason for my visit. She was puzzled, she had to confess. Was she to understand that the police were opening a new investigation into Ella's death? As I explained, she listened carefully, interjecting often to ask questions, until she felt she understood the situation. Then, brisk and organised, she began to talk. She remembered Ella very well, she said, she'd taught her

History. Early on, she was a good student, written work fine, contributions in class strong. Intelligent, no doubt about it, good in discussions, if always headstrong, a little too aggressive, even then. In due course, she was expected to go on to university.

She seemed ready to give me the reason why this had not happened, but I asked first if she had met Ella's foster-parents. She had. A good family, she said. True, Ella's mother had seemed rather colourless, one of those quiet, uselessly fussing people, but Ella's father she remembered as a forceful character, traditionalist in his views. He always took the lead at parents' evenings, wanting to know if his foster-daughter was knuckling down to work. He seemed proud of her, Ms Bell said, and also ambitious. He'd been to university himself – Nottingham rang a bell – and wanted the same for his daughter. She paused to reflect. Ella was forceful too, of course, like him, and it came out inappropriately at times, though it was surely a positive factor in certain areas, her sports, for instance. She was one of the very few athletes of national excellence that the school had produced and might have gone on to real success if she hadn't 'made mistakes'.

She was keen to tell me about the mistakes, but again I refused her cue and asked her instead if Ella had been popular with other students. Ms Bell thought about that for some time. Other students looked up to her, she said at last, because of her sporting abilities, although she didn't think Ella had close friends, she was never really part of a group. Now that she came to think of it, it was striking how Ella never played team sports but stuck to solo track and field events. She wouldn't describe Ella as isolated but rather that she carried with her a sense of herself as different or somehow apart.

Now, she went on without allowing any further interruption, I would obviously want to know about the incident that led to her exclusion. It was straightforward, if shocking. Ella, by then fourteen years old, attacked a fifth-form boy, two years older than herself. It happened during morning break on one of the playing fields, where the boy was relaxing with his friends. It was a serious assault: an ambulance was called and the boy spent the night in hospital with broken cheekbones. The school had been left with no alternative but to exclude Ella. The boy's father, Ms Bell added, happened to be a magistrate. I asked the obvious question but Ms Bell just shook her head. She had no idea why Ella had done it. It had been unprovoked. Ella herself refused to offer any explanation whatever. Ms Bell's own best guess was that the boy had disparaged her in some way – made comments about the fact that she was adopted or even about the colour of her skin – though the boy denied it and Ella in fact never claimed it. Of course, the real problem, she said, was Ella's temper, which, by this stage, had become uncontrollable. I asked about the boy. A large, solid boy, Ms Bell said, unremarkable, one of those boys who seem always to be in the background. Later, in fact, he was himself accused of mistreating a younger pupil, though by then he was at the end of his final term of sixth form. So perhaps those who suffer violence learn to pass it on to others, she said.

She went on about Ella. The assault wasn't the first time she'd been in trouble. Shortly before that, she'd been accused of stealing sports equipment from the gym. I remembered Ella's foster-mother mentioning it and asked Ms Bell to explain. Ella often trained late on her own at the school, she said, both on the track and in the gym, and was allowed to use the school's equipment so long as she replaced it and locked up when she left. Frankly, it was too much responsibility to have given a child, and it had been no surprise to Ms Bell when various items went missing; weights, she seemed to remember, and starting blocks. There was no question that Ella had taken them, for the missing things were found at her home, but the sports master subsequently withdrew his accusation, wanting to give Ella the benefit of the doubt and, Ms Bell supposed, defer to their outstanding athlete. Personally, Ms Bell felt that it sent the wrong signal. Young people do not benefit from a sense of entitlement. Like other teachers, she felt Ella's behaviour required closer supervision, a view sadly vindicated when the assault happened almost immediately afterwards. But, she went on, there was no doubting Ella's athletic abilities or her extraordinary dedication. Ms Bell had witnessed this herself. In the winter, when it was dark and cold, as she left the building after working late she had frequently encountered Ella on the track, and would often stop to watch her as she repeated her training exercises over and over again, a shadow in the darkness moving repetitiously to and fro, her footsteps suddenly popping on the asphalt and falling silent and exploding into life again. She was truly a remarkable athlete, Ms Bell said, and what had struck her most was Ella's dedication, her determination; there was a sort of ferocity about it, a refusal to be satisfied. Perhaps all successful athletes have this, she reflected, this fury to succeed; Ella certainly had it, but in her case such insatiability or fury could be misdirected, as had happened in the assault and also, not to put too fine a point on it, in her later life, which, as I knew, had been blighted by violence and the self-violence of addiction.

We sat for a moment in silence. She asked me if I had any more questions.

What had happened to the boy Ella had assaulted, I

wondered. Ms Bell didn't see the point of this question but she merely raised an eyebrow and answered. He went on to university somewhere.

And the younger pupil the boy was later accused of mistreating?

She saw the point of this even less but, as before, she remembered. She moved away, she said. Her father was also a teacher at the school, the sports master in fact, and he took a post at another school down south somewhere.

Thinking again about Ella, she became thoughtful. Those winter evenings, when she watched Ella practising alone on the track, something else had struck her apart from Ella's determination. Her loneliness. Ella always trained alone. It made her think now that she must have been a very inward person, alone with her thoughts for long periods, which would require a great deal of mental discipline. What would happen to her when she lost her purpose as an athlete, Ms Bell wondered. She speculated sadly that, when her discipline broke down, Ella had been overwhelmed by confusion and fear. In all her years at Whirlowdale, Ms Bell said, Ella showed not the slightest interest in boys. Yet, later, as she understood it, she became a prey to men. How strange, she mused, and terrible, that someone so independent and smart and resourceful and determined, so assertive, should become so helpless, too weak to escape their abuse. Drugs were of course a big part of it. But did Ella's rage to succeed turn to rage against herself in some strange way?

She had become thoughtful and sombre. 'We teach success at this school,' she said. 'We take our failures very hard.'

After I left her, while waiting for my taxi outside, I walked across the staff car park to the school's athletics track and stood for a time watching pupils with a sports master, and, as I watched them huddling together, drifting away into position, talking and laughing with each other, a frivolous group at ease with itself, I thought of Ella training there alone in the darkness, in a fury of concentration, as Ms Bell had described it, exemplifying the school's ethos of attainment, in fact. Then my taxi arrived and I asked the driver to take me back into the city.

It was the busiest time of day at the café on the corner of Edward Street and Scotland Street, lunchtime customers filling the tables inside and spilling out on to the blazing pavement. In the mornings it was much quieter, mainly serving takeaway drinks for construction guys working on nearby sites, and at night – it stayed open until midnight – very quiet indeed, the only customers a few last drunks, occasional sex workers, and the odd student taking a break from an all-nighter. But now it was full. Dean Burton had already arrived and was waiting for me with a cappuccino at the counter behind the plate-glass window, his favourite place, he told me at once, he loved to watch the streets, he was a people watcher and a 'people person', he said, that was the way he was made. He didn't add, 'Take it or leave it,' but he might have done. He was a small man in early middle age with an overlarge head on a delicate neck, his features set close together in his pale face, regular but indistinct; and although it was such a hot day he wore a sleeveless sweater over the top of his shirt, corduroy trousers and a flat cap. Also sunglasses. He was a car mechanic at a small local garage but this relaxed gentleman-at-leisure style was clearly his 'look'. He was a Sheffielder through and through, he said, still living in the house in Woodseats, where he grew up in, not far from Jordanthorpe, where Caine lived, though 'a step up', as Dean put it, a quiet area with some good pubs and Graves Park, one of the biggest parks in Sheffield. As if to demonstrate his origins, he spoke with a strong Sheffield accent, flattened vowels and softly bitten-off consonants, and had a habit, while speaking, of smiling, as if on the verge of saying something funny, which, however, he never did. He was keen to tell me that he was a regular customer at the café, particularly at night, and indeed a well-known figure in the area, where, several times a week, he spent what he coyly called his 'leisure hours'.

As he talked, he became lively with a sense of his own importance, excited at finding himself in a position to help the police with their inquiries, as he had helped them before, five years earlier, in identifying the man he encountered in Upper Allen Street as Michael Godley. Soon he was telling his story of that evening, beginning with an account of his visit to a massage parlour at about 9.00 p.m., where, he said without embarrassment, he was a regular, known to all the girls. He broke off from his narrative, in fact, to speak enthusiastically about sex work, which he considered a service no less respectable than any other, more so in fact, since it brought relief and pleasure to men like himself and provided the girls with a career. He challenged me to disagree with this, but I asked him instead if he'd ever used the services of the women who solicited on the streets: Ella Bailey, for instance. He struck a pose of regret. When he was young, he said, and not so wise, he added, he'd resorted to 'street girls' but soon discovered them to be a different class of person altogether, often addicts, crude and unhelpful and likely to be diseased. They fought each other, he added, and were often beaten by their managers, and he couldn't get pleasure from a girl with a black eye or bleeding mouth. Personally, he found physical injuries off-putting. At the parlour, he said, it was very different, he got a cup of tea and choice of biscuits as soon as he arrived, and while he waited for the girls to ready themselves for him he could chat to the owner, a sensible woman who kept tropical fish, as he did. He treated the girls with respect, he said, and was respected in return. The rooms were comfortable and clean, he added, and one of them had a jacuzzi.

No, he said at last in answer to my question, he didn't think he'd ever had anything to do with Ella Bailey.

I asked him to tell me what he'd done after leaving the massage parlour the evening she disappeared and he told me he'd come to the café for a chat, though he found no one to talk to, and, at about 11.30 p.m., feeling hungry, he'd walked round to Upper Allen Street to see if the balti house was still open. It wasn't, so he thought he'd call it a night and walk back to his car which he'd left, as usual, further down the street. But as he set off he heard a noise in the little alley next to the balti house. This was his moment of drama now, and he narrated what had happened next second-by-second, becoming animated, his eyes widening as he talked. The sudden noise in the darkness startled him – he cocked his head for me, assuming a puzzled expression, to act out his reaction at the time. A scuffling, he said, making a scuffling noise through pursed lips. He thought it might be an animal, perhaps a rat, but almost immediately he heard a second noise, a sharp exhalation of breath, cough-like, certainly human. He imitated this noise too, a dry retching, then assumed a shocked expression to show his surprise. He'd stopped and peered into the alley. It was too dark to see anything, however. He'd called out. This too he mimed, cupping a hand round his mouth. 'Hello? Someone there?' No answer. And then, just as he was about to move off, a figure emerged. A man, he said, materialising in front of him, zipping up his flies. Still only a shadow, this man took a cigarette out of his mouth, tossed it aside, and spoke a few indistinct words, coming into view out of the darkness, hunched a little as he walked, keeping his eyes on Dean, walking past him without further acknowledgement, turning into Upper Allen Street and going away in the direction of Scotland Street. 'Godley,' Dean said, and this was the punchline, in need of no elaboration, and he dropped his eyes modestly.

I asked if, all these years later, he was still confident in his identification. As he'd just said, it had been dark, Godley's beanie was pulled down low.

Dean dismissed these objections at once. Godley had passed by him no more than a metre away, he'd seen him clearly. Every detail of his story was exact, he said; and he went through it all again: Godley emerging, Godley zipping up his flies, Godley taking the cigarette out of his mouth, Godley speaking, Godley walking hunched. Every tiny bit of it was imprinted on Dean's memory, he saw it all now as he'd seen it that night, he said.

I'd read a transcript of Dean's court room testimony and observed that in the trial he hadn't said anything about Godley smoking a cigarette. Now he became flustered. Not at the trial, he said, no, at the trial the cigarette was an irrelevant detail, the judge had specifically asked all wit-nesses to stick to the essential facts. But it was true, he would testify to it. 'Under oath,' he added indignantly. Anyway, he repeated, although it had been dark, he'd seen Godley clearly and recognised him as soon as he'd been shown a photograph of his face. An ordinary-looking face, he said, nothing interesting about it, but one which he would never forget.

He settled into a blinking silence, a childish pout on his face.

After a few moments, he recovered enough to ask me if there was anything else I wanted to ask him. It was clear, in fact, that he wanted to prolong our conversation. That chance encounter in Upper Allen Street five years earlier had been a special moment for him, a public-facing moment, and when he talked about it he became a little larger in his voice and body language as if he felt a new respect for himself.

I asked if he still believed Ella had died that night. He was one hundred per cent sure of it. Now he became expan-sive. Killed and dumped in a bin, he said, the evidence presented at the trial left no room for doubt. There was no way out of that alley. And her killer was Godley, hard evidence proved it, not just Dean's own testimony but the CCTV, the police ANPR record of Godley in the area, his previous murders, not to mention his eventual confession. To be honest, he said – dropping his voice and leaning towards me conspiratorially – he'd *felt* it at the time. As Godley had passed by him, he felt the hairs on the back of his neck rise up. Naturally, he'd not mentioned this at the trial, the court room is a place for nothing but facts, but he could tell me now, he said, man to man. It was a physical sensation, a revulsion triggered not only by Godley but also the stinking darkness out of which he'd emerged, a sense of something not human, the presence of death, the murdered body of Ella Bailey, he meant, in the bin.

He fell momentarily silent, it seemed as a mark of respect.

I asked him then about the recent murder and he began to talk again, more agitated but at the same time more dismissive. This was not 'his' murder. In his opinion, the killer was probably from out of town: a murder was a very un-Sheffield thing. People in Sheffield were not like that. The only other murder he could think of was the one committed by Godley – and he was from Wakefield. On the evening of this new murder, Dean had been in Mexborough visiting his mother and as the news came on she'd been as shocked as he was to hear about it, and immediately fearful for her son's safety in the city. In fact, the killing had already disrupted his life, he said. Although it had happened on the streets, the girls whose company he enjoyed in the parlours were alarmed too, and one of them had actually moved away from the area and was no longer available. He hoped the police would act promptly to get things back to normal, and he asked me with evident anxiety if the investigation was proceeding at speed. He'd heard that they'd managed to obtain some forensic information from the body of the murdered girl. Was it true? What sort of evidence? He was keen to engage me on the matter, asking about the sorts of microscopic fibres and hairs and other things from which science can now extract DNA and other incriminating matter, but I said, as soon as I could, that I had no information about the case, and he fell silent, although I could see that he disbelieved me. The childish pout returned but I pacified him by asking if, with his deep knowledge of the area, he might be able to give me the name of any sex worker still in the area who had known Ella. He reminded me that he didn't have anything to do with the girls who worked the streets. Nor did the girls in the parlours, he added. Street girls were a different breed, as he'd already told me. But I could tell that he wanted to be helpful – as he had been five years earlier – and he gave it thought for a while without much result. The problem was that there was such a large turnover in girls working the streets, he said, they got into trouble or were driven away by other girls or simply disappeared, and five years was a long time, most street girls from so far back had long gone from St Vincent's. He frowned into his empty cappuccino cup and at last spoke. There was a girl who worked up Scotland Street and came into the café late at night. Frankly, he'd no idea if she'd known Ella, but she might be worth trying, she'd been around for a long time. Her name was Lauren but people called her Loz. He had to warn me, however, that she was unlikely to tell me the truth, or even make much sense; and he told me firmly that I should be careful not to give her money for her information, she would certainly spend it on drugs. Like nearly all the street girls, she was a junkie. In fact, now he thought about it, he hadn't seen her for a while, it was possible she was dead. I would find out, I said, and thanked him and told him how helpful he'd been, and he insisted on giving me his contact details in case I had other questions. I said I had just one more. Had he eaten often at the balti house on Upper Allen Street? Yes, he said, it had been one of his regular spots, it was a real shame it had closed down. Another disruption to his leisure hours. I asked if he knew what had happened to the staff and he told me he was friendly with one of the waiters, Karim, who now worked in another restaurant near the university, where the tandoori wasn't at all bad, and if I went there I should mention his name to Karim, I'd be given special treatment. Again, he was pleased with himself, and decided to stay in the café a little longer and perhaps have another cappuccino, and I left him there at the window, looking at ease with himself despite the darkness he had encountered.

He was a bore of course and also untrustworthy, not a deliberate liar but a man whose self-importance made him invent things to fit his myth. However, both bores and the delusional can be interesting, or at least suggestive, in their elaborations, and as I walked up Edward Street to my Airbnb I wondered if he'd been right about Godley's cigarette. So far as I knew, Godley had not been a smoker.

The long northward road towards Barnsley rises and falls over the bricked-over Sheffield hills, passing through stone remnants of old villages and zones of car showrooms to arrive finally at the Northern General Hospital, a spacious campus of low-rise barracks-like buildings sitting above the packed roofs of Fir Vale's red-brick terraces and the green treeline of woods bordering Firth Park. It was here that Lauren Gissing, called Loz, had been brought in an ambulance the previous week, something I'd eventually discovered from her social worker. My taxi dropped me off and I went inside to find Dr Elmira Hussein, who was looking after her.

I do not like hospitals. During the terrible days after the car crash in France, I developed a horror of them, sitting numbly hour after hour in my hospital smock in the little white room where my wife and son lay among the machines that were temporarily keeping them alive. Everything had been quiet and somehow remote, as if I were no longer connected to what was around me. The only noises were the tiny electronic blips and the soft footsteps and sympathetic voices of the medical staff. I was alone in my mind with the picture of the long, ongoing road and sudden black bulk of the lorry appearing out of the blue sky. My only feelings were of terror and guilt, my only thought the idea that I would resign all my future happiness, every tiny scrap of it, if they were only allowed to live, a bargain I fervently swore with all my stubborn, unyielding nature, though such intense mental effort was unsustainable and, besides, in the end, the bargain was not accepted. It had never been mine to make.

At the end of all the nauseating corridors and little white rooms, I found Dr Hussein in a cafeteria, where she was taking a break between shifts, a handsome woman with a thick mane of hennaed hair and splendid nose. She looked at me with curiosity when I spoke.

'*Min Baghdad?*'

Yes, I said, I was from Baghdad. Mansur.

'*Mansur! Mantaqa raqia jiddan. Ana min al Yarmouk.*'

She had grown up in Yarmouk, the district next to

Mansur, I remembered it well from my childhood, and so, unexpectedly, our conversation began with reminiscences of our home city. Like me, she had grown up in a wealthy family and spoke first of visits to exclusive spots I would recognise, the al Sa'ah restaurant on 14th Ramadan Street, the al Rasheed Hotel, the Iraqi Hunting Club, though her childhood, like mine, was actually a matter of home and school, and her most constant memories, which she went on to mention, were vaguer and more personal: heat rising in the garden, the sound of water, a room, a book, idle adventures with a long-lost friend. Although she'd never gone back, she could imagine returning, and in fact often dreamed of it, walking up the front steps of her old house, passing through the door, finding her room again – with everything in it intact, she said, laughing, even the book she had been reading still lying on the bed where she left it all those years ago. She was ten years younger than me but had stayed in Iraq longer and remembered the build-up to the invasion, the closed shops and anxious rallies in Liberty Square, before her parents, both doctors, brought her away, to Britain. She wanted to know when I'd left Iraq, and I told her it was not long after the end of the First Gulf War. By then, well aware of the dangers ahead, my parents were pessimistic about the country's future, though in the end it was not, I said, the mass deaths of civilians in the Al'Amariya shelter in 1991 that finally convinced them to send me abroad, but the closure of the Baghdad ice-cream parlours two years later – so, as it turned out, my safety owed more to sugar rationing than American bombs. In return, Dr Hussein told me that for years after she'd arrived in Britain as a young child, her parents continued to insist that one day they would all return to Iraq, to their house in Yarmouk, in fact, with the result that Britain had never seemed home, even now, she said, when she was married to an Englishman and had a daughter at school. Perhaps I too had a family here, she said. I shook my head. Then, she said, smiling, one day maybe I would go back to Mansur and live there again; and if I did, she added, I should think of her when I walked down Four Streets.

At last, I explained what I wanted to talk to her about. She saw plenty of missing people in the hospital, she said after a moment. Not officially missing, of course, missing socially, psychologically, emotionally, missing somehow from their own lives, as if real life had gone on without them and they had been left behind, bewildered and lost, trapped by addiction or violence or poverty, with no way to find themselves again. Lauren Gissing was such a person, she said.

I asked if Lauren had been admitted to hospital after an

overdose. Not this time, Dr Hussein said, no. She'd been attacked in the street and brought unconscious first to A&E, then to the Injuries Unit, where Dr Hussein – a specialist in trauma – had been looking after her. Her skull was fractured, her arm broken, and her recovery had been retarded by weaknesses in her constitution undoubtedly made worse by her addiction. On arrival, she'd been in a very weakened and confused state. Only slowly had she begun to make a recovery, a process not helped by the fact that she was such a defenceless, agitated person, who found it difficult to settle and impossible to accept medical advice of the simplest sort, which was frustrating, especially as Lauren had told her that she'd once trained as a nurse. Also, Dr Hussein said, she was frightened, almost to the point of paranoia, always assuming the worst about others – she claimed, for instance, that her phone had been stolen from her bedside – and fearful of life in general, which was hardly surprising, she supposed, given the nature of her work. She was always in conflict about something. As it happened, she was filing a complaint against the hospital, which, although baseless and ridiculous, would have to go through the system, wasting Dr Hussein's time with paper-work, interviews and perhaps even an appearance in front of a disciplinary committee.

Sympathising with her, I asked if she knew anything

about the attack on Lauren. Very little, she said. It had happened in the street somewhere in St Vincent's. At night? No, Lauren had arrived at the hospital in the middle of the afternoon. To find out more, though, I would need to talk to Lauren herself. Before I did that, I said, I'd be interested to know if Lauren had had many visitors in hospital. Dr Hussein was aware of only three. Friends, she assumed. Two were young women – perhaps, to be frank, also sex workers – who had come separately, each bringing alcohol with them, which had to be confiscated. And a man, she said, also young, though running to seed, wearing a white vest and fedora hat. I showed her a photo of Caine Poynton-Smith. Yes, she said, that's him. He'd told her he was there to try to cheer Loz up.

I thanked her for all her time and asked her to direct me to the ward where Lauren was, and she looked at me, surprised. There was a misunderstanding: Lauren had discharged herself a few hours earlier. She hadn't even waited to talk to Dr Hussein but had disappeared immediately after her final visitor, this Caine, had been with her. Just vanished. In fact, Dr Hussein had assumed the missing person I'd said I was looking for was Lauren. Was there a problem? Was she at risk? I asked if her sudden unauthorised departure from hospital had been reported to the police and she looked at me sadly. Did I think they had time to report it every time a patient left without approval?

She walked with me, back through the corridors to the exit, and wished me luck. I shouldn't worry too much about Lauren disappearing like that, she said. Sudden departures were probably a feature of her life, and we shouldn't forget that departures in general are a feature of everyone's lives, sometimes sudden, sometimes long-delayed, sometimes trivial, sometimes profound. Think of us, she said. We left behind one part of the world to arrive the next minute in another entirely new one, to begin everything again, and who is to judge the different degrees of dislocation in all these disappearances? We are a restless species, she said. Nowhere is home. And in that sense Lauren is merely typical.

It took me half an hour to get Lauren's address, and another twenty minutes to get to Edward Street, in St Vincent's, where she lived. The old low-rise apartment buildings were arranged in a loop around a central grassy garden, with shared walkways hung now with washing, and many entrances and stairwells. There was a frustrating delay in finding Lauren's flat and, when I got there, there was no answer to my knock, no sign of occupation at all.

The lady in the neighbouring flat told me that she hadn't

seen Loz for weeks. But I wasn't the first to come round banging on her door either, she said, sometimes in the middle of the night. I asked her if she had seen the person who had done this banging, and she said she hadn't, she'd only heard them, a male voice very loud and angry; and I thanked her and went back to my Airbnb.

I sat in the perfect, sterile living room of my apartment with my laptop, thinking about Loz, and where she might be, and about Caine Poynton-Smith, the odd manner in which he'd answered some of my questions, the coincidence of him going up to the hospital to see Loz immediately after I'd talked to him. After a while, I looked through the various reports DS Nunkoo had sent me. I rewatched the CCTV footage from Upper Allen Street and tried to see if 'Godley' had been smoking as he came out of the alley but the images were too dark to be conclusive.

A little while later, Nunkoo called with answers to the questions I'd sent her earlier. The boy whom Ella attacked at Whirlowdale School had died in his first year of university in a motorbike accident. The girl whose father had been sports master had relocated to France in her early twenties and her current whereabouts were unknown. However, she went on, she had one positive piece of information: she could tell me for certain that Michael Godley was never a smoker. He was in fact asthmatic. His wife and GP had confirmed it. What did it mean, she wanted to know, and I explained. It confirmed her suspicion that Godley was not Ella Bailey's assailant, but I warned her that Dean Burton was not a trustworthy source, and we both felt, in fact, that it was too early to jump to conclusions. In the end, she simply asked me for an update in due course, and in return I asked her to keep trying to locate the girl who went to France and to let me know if any report concerning Lauren Gissing came her way.

I went back to thinking about Godley. Either Dean Burton had invented the cigarette – quite possible, I thought – or he'd seen another man that night. A smoker. Like, for instance, Caine Poynton-Smith. Eventually, though, I grew tired and, closing my laptop, began to drift round the pristine apartment, not thinking of anything at all, just looking. As a boy in Baghdad I was prone to fits of such dreaminess: my teachers at school used to say, 'Talib has difficulties concentrating.' As I sat in the bedroom, letting my mind wander, I noticed something under the corner of the bed. It was a wax earplug, obviously missed by the cleaner, and now, in the sanitised, apparently memoryless apartment, a rare trace of previous occupation, something human, grubby and weirdly intimate, a glob of pink wax squished into the shape of someone's inner ear. It reminded me of Dr Hussein's idea of returning to Iraq and finding some trace of herself in her old family home in Yarmouk, an actual fragment of her childhood, the book she'd been reading lying on her bed – though, like the earplug, what she found could equally well turn out to be something disconcerting. Of course, the idea of finding any such object from her former life was a fantasy. What Dr Hussein would actually find, and in abundance, were memories. As soon as she re-entered the house, they would come flooding back, both true and false, things she had forgotten, things she had invented, but all of them real to the person she had become, intimate, like all memories, perhaps sometimes grubby too. And I thought again of Dean's memory of Ella's attacker's cigarette.

At last, I took my book and went out into the streets and walked towards the university district, where I eventually found the restaurant Dean had mentioned to me. The waiter Karim wasn't there, however, he was on leave, returning the next day, though I stayed to eat anyway and Dean had been right, the tandoori wasn't at all bad. While I ate, I read Chapter 8 of *Persuasion*, which describes a dinner party at the house of Charles Musgrove, Anne Elliot's brother-in-law. Here, eight years after turning down undistinguished Fred Wentworth's proposal of marriage, Anne meets him again – now Captain Wentworth, successful and eligible – and, though she is still in love with him, polite manners require her to quietly stand aside while other, younger women – giggly Louisa and Henrietta Musgrove – vie to attract his interest. As Puck had pointed out, these were the rules of competition in the nineteenth-century marriage market. But what struck me was the demure Anne's fierce determination to play by those rules, to deliberately put that code of conduct above her self-interest.

By the time I'd finished my meal, it was 7.00 p.m., still too early for what I intended to do, so I went back to my Airbnb and, as I was letting myself into the apartment, the door opposite opened, exactly as before, and the young student called Puck stood there. It was like a replay of our earlier meeting. I said I still wasn't the person she was expecting, and she said she still wasn't expecting anyone, and asked me how I was getting on with *Persuasion*, and we exchanged thoughts about books. 'What's the point of stories, really?' she asked. I said something about empathy. She liked style in writing, she said, style held everything together, and in fact I could tell that style was important to her, the style of her loose clothes, cropped hair, tongue-in-cheek manner and provocative comments; all these things, I thought, were consciously adopted styles. I commented, as I had before, that she was living in an unusually fancy place for a student, and to my surprise she invited me in to see it, and this too seemed a part of her style, a determined carelessness, a conspicuous refusal anyway to abide by social norms which advised against an eighteen-year-old girl living alone inviting a strange man in his mid-forties into her place at night.

Her apartment was even larger than my own, with a much more spacious living room and, she told me, three bedrooms. One of them was full of photographic paraphernalia, tripods, screens, light projectors, which were necessary for her university project, she said: her chosen medium was video. It was useful to have the extra space. 'Daddy pays,' she said. She hadn't seen her father for almost a year, she added as she made coffee, but he was a good payer. 'Guilt and money,' she said. 'What else is there?' As it turned out, it was also part of her style to talk about the most intimate aspects of her life, her mental health issues, for instance, her parents' divorce, even her sexuality. She felt passionately about issues of personal identity and was angered by the violent discriminatory attacks on trans and neurodiverse people and, even now, on Black and brown people. She was proud to have close friends from these groups and stood with them against prejudice. I asked her if she knew any poor people and she said no. They fall into the category of 'hard to reach', she said after a moment. Throughout our conversation I was conscious of how young she was, still a child in many ways, if precocious, a Gen Z, one of the so-called 'snowflake generation', though in no way a snowflake herself. She was spunky and smart and fiercely opinionated, and I liked her. She could be alarming, though. Just as she revealed the most personal details about herself without a qualm, she asked me the most provocative, in fact invasive, questions without the slightest sense of trespass. Where did I come from? What was I doing in Sheffield? Who was I really? She didn't believe I was a businessman, she said with a smile.

I told her I was with the police, a finder, and I was looking for a sex worker, though it was possible, I admitted, that she was no longer alive. She regarded me coolly. Well, I'd come to the right place, she said. Plenty of sex workers here. I asked her if she wasn't nervous living in a red-light district, and she gave a little shrug. She didn't get nervous, she said. Not that type. I wondered out loud if her father might get nervous on her behalf, particularly after the recent murder. She ignored that and began to talk about the women who worked the streets. She wanted to know why we stigmatised them. Think of *Persuasion*, she said. Was the marriage market Austen described so different from the sex market? They're both markets, money changes hands, the women compete for it, fight according to the rules, polite or crude depending. Sexual politics 101, she said. She was definite and provocative in the manner of the young. I asked her if she'd talked to any of the women who worked in the area. Certainly she had, she liked to go down to the café where they hung out late at night and talk to them. Daddy wouldn't approve, she added, with obvious satisfaction, and I wondered how much of what she did was motivated by her desire to annoy her father.

I produced a photograph of Lauren Gissing and showed it to her. Yes, she said, she'd seen her around, though not for a while and had never talked to her. I showed her a photograph of Caine Poynton-Smith and she looked at it for a long time. Perhaps, she said at last. Has he got a squint? Did he carry a red kitbag? She'd seen someone similar with such a bag and thought perhaps he was a pimp, or maybe a dealer, though she couldn't say for certain. She handed back the picture. Good luck with finding the woman, she said.

By now it was late and I said I should go. She saw me to the door, like a middle-aged matron.

'How often do you actually find the people you look for?' she asked. 'Often enough to make it worthwhile?'

I said that it was always worthwhile to the one I found, and she smiled, a little wistfully I thought, and closed the door, and I waited a moment to hear her footsteps recede on the other side of it, then turned away from my apartment and went out of the building into the night.

It was dark outside but still warm and I walked first to St George's Park and looked round. There were still plenty of people about, mainly students, wandering to and fro, or sitting on the low walls talking. Sly's body had been found in bushes bordering the lawn, almost in full view, and I wondered why her killer would take such a risk. It suggested overwhelming emotion, some rage or desperation. On my way out of the park I encountered Flynn the vagrant who recognised me and wiggled his fingers in my direction. 'Hey, Walt.' It seemed to be his standard greeting as well as his own response. I asked him to show me the bench where he thought he'd seen Ella, and he became confused, taking me first to one bench then another. It didn't seem to be there anymore, he said at last, sorrowfully. But he brightened at the thought of her sitting on it. She giggled and laughed, he told me. She was in a good place. She was dead, he added, and gave me a look both sad and quizzical.

He began to rummage in a nearby bin and I thanked him and moved on, back towards St Vincent's. At night, it was more desolate than ever, long vistas of empty dark lots, silent fenced-off construction sites and, here and there, the tall silhouettes of student blocks. But, although it was 8.00 p.m., the café was still open. I wondered if I might find Dean Burton but he was not there, only two young women sitting at a table near the back. Neither was Loz. They told me that they didn't know her, nor Caine Poynton-Smith, nor a man with a red kitbag, so I got a coffee and sat at the counter in the window, where I'd sat before, to watch the street. There was very little to watch, however; Scotland Street was deserted. The two young women talked in low voices about someone called Diss or Tiss, who was pregnant, and after half an hour they left and I went over to talk to the café owner. He was a Greek with a paunch and moustache, and he chewed something continually, a stoical, unsurprised expression on his face. His name was Andreas Georgoulas. Yes, he knew Loz. What had she done now? I explained why I wanted to talk to her and a little about my brief to find Ella Bailey, if she was still alive. He only grunted from time to time, placidly chewing. He hadn't seen Loz in several days, he'd heard she'd had an accident. Ella was dead, he said, despite having found her bag hanging on his door handles. If someone hadn't killed her back then, he said, she would have died some other way, she had a death wish. Threw it all away. Kid like that, he said, smart, funny. He shook his head. Drugs. That boyfriend of hers. He didn't know her, he added, never wanted to; besides, he made it a point of not getting over-friendly with his customers.

I asked him if Caine Poynton-Smith came into the café and if he'd ever seen him carrying a red kitbag. He didn't come anywhere near the café, Andreas said, he'd banned him. Flaky, he said. Liable to lose control. He didn't elaborate. Still looking at me, he rolled whatever he had in his mouth on to his tongue and spat it neatly into a bin. If I was interested in finding Loz, he went on, I should take a look up Shepherd Street or, failing that, in the streets around Kelham Island, over the dual carriageway. With that, he turned away, and I left him and went out to continue my search.

I found no one.

It was 10.00 p.m. by the time I returned from Kelham Island and before going back to my Airbnb I thought I might as well go round to the Edward Street flats and knock on Loz's door one more time, just in case. Which was a good decision, because she was there.

Unlike the new student blocks, the Edward Street flats are old, and old-fashioned, but they were built by the council in a more civic age and Loz's flat was surprisingly spacious inside. At first she did not want to let me in. She shouted at me to go away, threatened to set her dog on me (she did not have one) and fetch her brother to sort me out (he was in Guatemala). But once I persuaded her that I was not there to collect on a debt, she opened the door. She didn't like a row, she said, though her life, she added, had seemed like nothing so much as one long argument. She told me straight away that she never talked to the police on principle, and I explained that I wasn't the police. She said then that there was no point talking to her anyway, because she'd always had problems concentrating, and she was even worse now because someone had just tried to kill her and she was, in her own words, 'all over the fucking shop', and I told her I would be very patient, and, at last, still grumbling, she led me into the front room.

She was a small woman in her late twenties, already starting to age and shrink. Unsurprisingly, she looked a mess. One side of her head had been shaved and was covered by a dressing; her left arm was in a sling. She wore an overlarge woollen jumper over the top of her hospital smock, which she seemed to have forgotten to take off, and her thin bare legs, visible up to the top of her thighs, were discoloured by bruises. The room we sat in was also a mess, clothes, crockery and magazines piled up round a couch, a chair and a bookcase with a dead potted plant and a photograph of a cat standing on its hind legs. 'Mascara,' she said, apparently the cat's name. The cat never appeared but I could smell it. As if surprised to find such disorder around her, she sat on the edge of the chair, hugging herself with her one good arm, peering about and scratching the dressing on her scalp. Her dark eyes were never still, moving restlessly in her pale face, and she grimaced from time to time, showing gums drawn back from her teeth. On the floor beside her was a bowl filled with sweets which she ate, one after another, urgently, without any apparent pleasure, fumbling with the orange wrappers which she dropped on to the floor. Sugar: the last resort of the addict who can't get hold of drugs.

The attack had obviously shaken her. I asked about her injuries and she said that she was lucky to be alive. The hospital had told her so, though the hospital, she added, was also criminally negligent and she was suing them. Did she have anyone who could be with her or at least look in from time to time? Embarrassed, she ignored the question. I mentioned that someone had been banging on her door at all hours, looking for her, and she frowned. Was it the woman next door told me that? Delusional, she said. Off her tits. Goes mental if she hears me breathing. As she spoke, a dog started barking nearby, a dull, hollow booming, and there were shouts from another direction, not harsh in tone but strident, and I thought the Edward Street flats must be one of those places which are never completely quiet. Distracted, she lit a cigarette, which she smoked while continuing to chew sweets. It had happened in broad daylight, she went on, meaning the attack. Middle of the afternoon. She couldn't believe it. She'd just got up and had gone out to buy a pint of milk from the filling station and was going down Solly Street and the next thing she knew there was this terrific thump on the back of her head and she was on the ground and her head felt like it was coming apart and someone was hitting her, kicking her, probably he had something with him, a bat or something, a bar, an iron bar perhaps, a tool of some sort, smacking her with it over and over in a sort of . . . what was that word, she couldn't think of the word. 'Frenzy,' I said. That's it, she said and blew out smoke. 'Fucking mental.' For a moment she was lost in the memory of it; she began to tremble, smoking hard in rapid snatches and speaking in gasps between puffs. Ever thought you were about to die? She was not looking for an answer. Weirdest feeling, she said. She frowned as she tried to put it into words. It was like, suddenly, nothing mattered, like there wasn't even anything else, anywhere, just her, on her own, the last little bit of her lying there, a speck on the pavement. Her most vivid memory of the attack was a crack in the paving stone which she saw as she lay with her face squashed on the ground, waiting to be killed. She shook her head in disbelief. 'Fucking mental,' she said again.

In her victim statement, she'd written that during the attack her assailant pulled her bag off her shoulder and I asked if the attack could have been a mugging. No, she said. Her purse was in her bag and he didn't take it, nor her phone, which was in her pocket, though that was taken later, she said, by some thieving bastard at the hospital. Besides, she'd been mugged before, several times, muggers only hurt you if you don't give them your stuff. This guy wanted to hurt her. If someone hadn't come down Meadow Street and seen it happening the guy wouldn't have stopped until she was dead. She glanced fearfully towards the door. There's a killer out there, she said. The guy who did Sly. She was convinced it was the same man. Sheffield wasn't safe anymore, she was going to have to get away, she had a cousin in Chesterfield and soon as she'd finished suing the hospital she was going to clear out till they caught him.

I asked if she remembered anything about her assailant. Nothing, she said. He'd come at her from behind, she hadn't even caught a glimpse of him. Did he say anything? She shook her head again. That was one of the weird things. Generally a guy can't stop screaming at a woman he's knocking about – bitch, whore, cow, whatever – but this guy didn't say a word, nothing, all she could hear was the sound of her own screams and the thud and crash of his blows.

I wondered out loud why that was. Could it be that if he spoke she might have recognised who it was?

She looked at me fearfully but said nothing.

I told her then that I'd been to the hospital and had talked to Dr Hussein. Now she looked at me warily. She thought I'd said I wasn't police.

I wanted to talk to her about Ella Bailey, I said. Dean Burton had told me that she used to know her. She sneered.

Dean Burton? Dean Burton was a joke, everyone knew that, the parlour girls made fun of him, even the street girls laughed at him. He had a nickname. 'Nappy'. Medical issues, she added, by way of explanation. You should see them bait him, she said, it drives him mental. Why did I want to talk about Ella Bailey anyway? She was getting confused. What had Ella Bailey to do with her attack?

Rather than explain my role again, I simply said that it was Ella I was interested in, and asked her what she could tell me about her. She was wary. Nothing much, she said. She used to see Ella around, up on Shepherd Street, sometimes in the café, only to talk to though, to swap tips, as girls do, pass on news about a punter, a cop, places to avoid. She hadn't known her well. She liked her alright, she was funny, she had a way with words. Of course, she had a bit of a habit too. Once Ella had lent her money, she said. That was nice. Another time she saw her fight a punter. She had a temper, Loz said.

She lit another cigarette from the butt of her last one, watching me. This about reopening the case then, she asked.

I didn't answer. I asked instead if she remembered making a statement to the police at the time of the investigation into Ella's disappearance. 'Vaguely,' she said. In it, I reminded her, she stated that she didn't know Ella at all, had hardly ever seen her and had never once talked to her. Loz shrugged. Always best to tell the police as little as possible, she said. Otherwise, in her experience, things could get out of hand.

I asked her what sort of things.

She put out her cigarette in a cup. It was getting late, she said. The hospital had told her to get plenty of rest. She glanced at her wrist as if to check the time, though she wasn't wearing a watch. Someone had stolen it, she said, same person who stole her phone, probably. Thing about people, she said, is they're lovely until they're twats. Like the people in the hospital, she added. She fell silent, twitching on the edge of her seat, anxious suddenly for me to leave. We watched each other for a moment or two, then I leaned over and showed her a photograph of Caine Poynton-Smith, and her face went stiff. He'd visited her in hospital earlier that day, I said, just before she discharged herself.

She opened her mouth and closed it again without speaking.

I asked her if he'd gone there to threaten her and she looked at me with the surprised, horrified expression of someone who has been found out and doesn't know what to do; and after a moment's resistance she collapsed and began to cry, quietly at first, then in great quaking bursts, and I went into the kitchen and fetched her a glass of water and waited until she was calm again. She was frightened, however, and still would not speak.

I told her that I'd visited Caine in the morning, and it seemed to me that my conversation with him had prompted him to go straight up to the hospital to see Loz. Why? To warn her against speaking to me? Although she said nothing, I could see from her face that this was the case, so I asked her what it was he didn't want her to tell me.

We had reached the point in the conversation when talk can either go forward or backward – but for a while Loz would not go anywhere, she was stuck, sitting on the edge of her chair, hugging herself, looking at me for help.

Alright, I said. Let me tell you then what I think happened.

She nodded, watching me expectantly, like a child listening to a story.

I think, I said, that, five years earlier, in the days just before she disappeared Ella had left Caine.

I could tell at once that I had guessed right. And it was, at last, the nudge Loz needed. She began to talk again, in a quiet voice, a whisper really, as if afraid of being overheard. Ella had come round to tell her. There had been nothing left in her relationship with Caine but drugs, arguments and fights. After months of talking about it, getting caught robbing had finally made Ella act.

Loz lit another cigarette and closed her eyes, remembering.

The night after Ella told her that, Caine turned up at the Edward Street flats. On the rampage, looking for Ella. Ella was going to tell the police lies about him and the robbery, he said. He didn't believe Loz that she wasn't in the flat and went through it room by room turning things upside down, and when he couldn't find her he suddenly lost it and started smashing things. He had a hammer, Loz said. She'd never been scared of him until then.

When was this?

The day before she was killed, she said.

She looked at me fearfully. I didn't need to point out to her that she hadn't mentioned any of this to the investigation at the time. She sat there biting her lip. It was clear that she was still frightened of Caine.

He came round again, she said, a few days after Ella disappeared. Panicking. He swore he hadn't done anything to her, warned Loz not to tell the police he'd been looking for her. And then, she went on, after all that, they got that other guy, that Godley, it turned out he was the one who did it, not Caine. She let out a huge sigh. Suddenly she had a lot more she wanted to say, about violent men and beaten women, selfish men and romantic women, but, although it was hardly off the point, I'd heard enough and thanked her for her time and went outside to call DS Nunkoo. But before I could dial, I noticed that Nunkoo had sent me a message, and I opened it. It told me that they'd just arrested Caine Poynton-Smith.

I sat in my Airbnb, glad of its silence and order after Loz's flat. Many things Loz had said puzzled me but it was late and I was too tired to sort them out so I sat on the pristine sofa and read Chapter 12 of *Persuasion*, which contains the famous scene in which Louisa Musgrove flirtatiously flings herself off the steep flight of steps of the Cobb at Lyme Regis, expecting Wentworth to catch her, and, taking him by surprise, crashes instead on to the pavement. What interested me was Anne's reaction. It is she who immediately organises help, calling for salts, sending someone for a surgeon, undertaking to tend to Louisa herself at the inn – all this for her rival in love. It was another example of her instinctive, even thoughtless, self-sacrificing conduct.

I woke thinking about the attack on Loz in Solly Street. She said she thought her assailant was Sly's killer attempting another murder, but to attempt murders on two consecutive days would be unheard of for a serial killer, who typically leaves a cooling-off period between attacks, and though a so-called 'spree killer' or 'rampage killer' may kill several people in rapid succession, I did not think the St Vincent's attacks fitted the pattern of incoherence and mess associated with such killings. Was it after all a violent (and unsuccessful) mugging? If so, what had they been after? And what about the assailant's silence – was it a tactic to avoid Loz recognising him?

Assuming, of course, that the assailant was a man.

Thinking these things, I dressed and went out into

another hot day. I had my breakfast at the Edward Street café, where Andreas behaved as if he'd never seen me before; then I took a taxi to join DS Nunkoo in Carbrook, where she was preparing to interview Caine Poynton-Smith. He was in custody there on suspicion of murdering Sly Stones. His false alibi (that he had been in Birmingham) had been exposed by newly discovered CCTV footage from a cashpoint near Sheffield Cathedral at 9.30 p.m., just two hours before Sly's murder at nearby St George's Park, in which he is seen with Sly, aggressively demanding the money she was withdrawing.

Before the interview, which I was to observe, I had a chance to update Nunkoo about my recent conversation with Loz; and at the end of our brief discussion she suggested I talk to Caine myself about Ella after she'd finished questioning him about Sly.

Her questioning was soon underway and I watched it on a screen in the adjoining room with a DC and staff support officer. In the twenty-four hours since I'd seen him, Caine had changed. Now hunched and shrunk inside a loose-fitting denim jacket, his handsome face pouched after a sleepless night in custody, he was frightened, his expression veering between anxiety and spite. He was no longer cool, nor fully in control. He looked like a man who has been found out. Nunkoo began by showing him the footage from the cashpoint camera and calmly presenting a series of statements and incontrovertible deductions which not only destroyed his claim that he had been in Birmingham but also established his aggressive conduct towards the murdered woman on the night of her death. Sly had been killed at around 11.30 p.m; the cashpoint footage put him in the vicinity, with her, just two hours earlier. Caine, not calm at all, was at first petulant, then surly, finally pleading. This was the pattern throughout their conversation. Lacking the self-control to maintain his lies, he quickly sought excuses for what he'd done. Nor could he keep his emotions out of his face. He'd lied because he was frightened, he said, because he knew he wouldn't be believed – but he didn't sound believable now. Whenever his solicitor intervened to challenge DS Nunkoo's approach she merely rephrased her question and Caine continued to struggle. As she told them, she'd taken the opportunity that morning to talk to a punter friendly with both Caine and Sly, and, armed with the information he had given, she soon had Caine admitting to extorting money from Sly over a period of months. After an hour of Nunkoo's patient questioning, although he continued to maintain that his altercation with Sly at the cashpoint was the last time he'd seen her, he was in bad shape and his solicitor requested a break.

For a while, Nunkoo huddled at the other end of the

observation room with her team. New information had just arrived, she told me at last, from two witnesses saying they'd seen Caine pursuing Sly near St George's Park less than half an hour before she was killed. Another of his lies had just been exposed. But before she resumed her questioning, Caine's solicitor would allow his client to help me with my own inquiries. Over the last couple of days, she went on, she'd looked again at the transcript of Caine's interview made at the time of Ella's disappearance and noted how evasive and contradictory he'd been, claiming to have been out of Sheffield all week before other testimony forced him to change his story. He'd been asked to attend a second interview, in fact, before the discovery of the Upper Allen Street CCTV footage turned all their attention to Michael Godley. Nunkoo wanted to know what I thought now. Was it possible Caine had killed Ella? I said I thought it possible. Perhaps his answers to my questions would help us decide.

Although Caine had been briefed about my appearance he still looked confused to see me. He even forgot to sneer. I confused him further by asking if he had a red kitbag; his answer to this simple question made no sense, and it was hard to tell if he was being dishonest or simply forgetful. He was certainly afraid. I told him then that I knew Ella had left him a couple of days before her presumed murder and that he had gone looking for her in a fury. Caught by surprise, he stupidly began by denying it. He was not a quick thinker; confronted with what Loz had told me, his denials petered out, as they had done repeatedly before, to be replaced by angry excuses and justifications. Yes, he'd gone looking for Ella, and why not? I put it to him that he'd wanted to stop her giving the police information about the attempted armed robbery. He denied it, he meant her no harm, he said. I mentioned the hammer he'd been carrying with him, and for a moment he couldn't think of anything to say. Horror came into his face as if he began to realise how bad it might get for him. I asked him once again why he'd waited a week before reporting Ella missing and he made the mistake of repeating his original lie that he had been out of Sheffield. He was badly rattled and began to make silly mistakes. He claimed he hadn't been anywhere near St Vincent's on the evening of Ella's murder, forgetting testimony by Andreas Georgoulas that he'd visited his café early on. He repeated his original claim that he'd spent the rest of the night alone in a club in West Street, waiting for a friend who never showed up – but this time gave the name of a different club altogether. He even denied going to the Northern General Hospital the previous day to intimidate Loz, forgetting that he'd talked to Dr Hussein and other staff there. Several times his solicitor suggested he take another break but he was panicking, unable to listen to advice. I had seen many people break down in interviews but none so painfully; he'd been carrying his lies so long that they were very deep inside him and as they were exposed he seemed physically torn apart. Soon I began to expect him to make a confession. His final defence was to fall back on the outcome of the original trial: Michael Godley murdered Ella, he said, everyone agreed, all the evidence proved it, there had even been a witness at the scene who identified him. It was an interesting point, though not one he should have brought up. I told him that I had spoken to the witness, who would testify that the man he had seen in the alley that night was smoking a cigarette. Godley didn't smoke, I said. But Caine did.

There was silence.

I asked him to tell me what had really happened that night five years earlier and he broke down and wept. In a state of incoherent distress, he asked his solicitor what was going to happen to him now but, before he could answer, DS Nunkoo, who had been monitoring the interview, came into the room and asked me to step outside. She had a peculiar expression on her face. Without saying more, she took me into another room and began to run camera footage on a monitor there. The footage showed different views of the inside of a bus half full of passengers. It was the number 75 service, she said, running on a route through Sheffield between Shiregreen in the north and Batemoor in the south. Recorded five days ago, Nunkoo said.

After a few moments she stopped the footage. The frame showed part of the upper deck, half a dozen people in view, sitting separately in seats next to the windows. She pointed to one of them.

'That's Ella Bailey,' she said. 'Caine didn't kill her, Godley didn't either. She's not dead.'

Ella looked completely different from her last photograph, older of course and much healthier, but there was no mistaking the birthmark on her forehead nor the bag over her shoulder with its distinctive check pattern and fringes. It was Ella Bailey, alive and in Sheffield only five days earlier.

DS Nunkoo said several times she couldn't believe it, then in silence we watched Ella sitting there, just another passenger on a bus, alone, expressionless, gazing ahead of her at some far unmoving object or, more likely lost in her thoughts, like the others sitting around her, or perhaps, I thought, concentrating on something, an inward focus. Scenery of treetops and roofs passed by the windows in fits and starts, passengers got on and took their seats nearby, or got off, and Ella was motionless, staring ahead. Then the footage abruptly came to an end. Glitch in the system, Nunkoo said, that snippet of recording was all they had, ten minutes' worth.

She reran it several times and we studied it together. Ella's nose seemed to have been broken since the last photographs we'd seen of her. What looked like scar tissue disfigured her right cheek. Otherwise, she seemed unchanged. She did not look like a person in hiding: she was dressed in a short skirt and stockings, flimsy halter-neck top, overlarge beret and a pair of large round tinted glasses chequered in pattern to match her bag. When she boarded and took her seat we could see that she was wearing high heels.

Nunkoo commented that she looked like a sex worker. It was true.

I pointed out that she was wearing exactly what Flynn the delusional vagrant had said she was, even the hat.

I remembered from our earlier conversation that the number 75 bus went to Jordanthorpe, where Caine lived, and I asked if that's where Ella had been going. No, Nunkoo said, she'd boarded at Arundel Gate in the city centre, not far from St Vincent's, and was travelling in the opposite direction, north, towards Firth Park – though, because there was no footage of her alighting, it wasn't clear where her destination had been.

Five years ago, Nunkoo said, she was dead in an alley. What happened?

We talked about the footage from Upper Allen Street on the night of Ella's disappearance, how the dustbin lorry briefly obstructed the entrance to the alley. I said that in the two hours that followed, three vans and one construction truck had pulled up in the same position, with the same result, and in fact the truck, a longer vehicle, had also overlapped the edge of the camera's view. Was it possible, I asked, that someone attacked and left for dead might come to consciousness in the early morning and climb out of a bin, or get up from behind the pile of rubbish or lumber where they had lain unseen all night, and leave the alley while a parked vehicle was blocking the camera's view and stagger away in the still deserted street? Improbable? It required us only to imagine some toughness, a little luck, a coincidence and the inattention of the officers looking at the footage. The evidence of the phone signal merely proved that Ella's phone had still been in the bin. And perhaps there was an innocent reason for the extra weight that morning. All this was true, though we had no time to talk further. Nunkoo needed to press ahead with the investigation into Sly Stones's murder; she was confident now of bringing charges against Caine. My task was to find Ella, as in fact it always had been. After all, Nunkoo said, she's wanted for attempted armed robbery. That was true, of course, but I said there might be another reason to find her as soon as possible.

She paused at the door. What's that?

I said I thought she might be at risk.

Nunkoo raised an eyebrow.

I asked her why she thought Ella had reappeared in St Vincent's. Why now just after a murder? Whatever else she was, Ella Bailey was a person who went towards danger, who got herself into trouble. Headstrong, her foster-parents had said. She was the schoolgirl who marched across playing fields to physically confront an older boy, careless of the consequences. Nunkoo nodded, but she had to go. She asked if I would inform Ella's foster-parents and I said I would. And after that? I said I would go and eat lunch somewhere quiet where I could reflect. There was an Indian restaurant near the university. She knew it. Try the shashlik chicken, she said, then she was gone.

At Knowle Lane, we sat as before in the front room and, in the momentary silence that followed my announcement, I heard the play of the water feature in the garden outside, the cool sound of water on another hot day. Everyone has their own way of dealing with shock. Mary crumpled at once, Ted sat stony-faced. Neither believed me. It was only after they had watched the footage several times that they allowed themselves to think it might be true.

'God forgive me,' Mary said. 'All these years I thought she was dead.'

Frantically, she began to ask me questions, wanting to know where Ella had been and what she'd been doing and what had caused her reappearance and what it meant, and as I kept repeating that I had no answers, I could see their increasing anxiety. Ted demanded to see the footage again and again. All this was normal, for the truth is so often unsettling and full of ambiguities and, putting it bluntly, untrustworthy, but their questions were also mine and I could not answer them, all I could do was to clarify what we knew and what we didn't. I could tell that they sensed my own anxiety, and finally Mary asked if Ella was in any danger. I replied carefully that St Vincent's was unfortunately a dangerous place at present. Was there anyone here she might want to contact? Ted gave me a look and I told him that Caine Poynton-Smith was in custody, helping with inquiries. Anyone else? They could think of no one. Finally, I asked them if they had any idea where she might have been going on the number 75 bus, heading north towards Firth Park. They didn't. After a while Ted said that he used to take Ella to athletic meets in Firth Park when she was a girl. The memory upset him and he glowered again at the footage. 'Why is she dressed like that?' he asked suddenly. Short skirt, stockings, high heels. I said I didn't know. It was time to leave. Ted followed me to the door. He wanted to know if I thought Ella had been in Sheffield for the last five years. I said that to remain hidden in a place where so many people knew her would be difficult. After a moment he nodded.

'Then what's she doing here now?'

I said once again that I didn't know.

He fixed me with his bleak gaze a moment longer, then nodded again, and I watched him go back down the hall, then let myself out into the sunshine.

The Tandoori Pavilion was tucked between Falafel King and a Malaysian café in a strip of modest red-brick terracing overshadowed by taller buildings: a new university tower block, a church and a grand Victorian pub. Up the hill was the gleaming bulk of the city's children's hospital. In the middle of the afternoon, the restaurant was empty and I sat alone in the window watching students pass by, climbing the hill towards the arts tower or going into the pub.

As I ate my shashslik chicken, I thought about Ella Bailey. The mystery of her escape from that alley, whatever conjunction of luck and coincidence had made it possible, could wait. More urgent were the questions Ted had asked me. Where had she been for five years? Why was she dressed as a sex worker? More troubling still, why had she come back to Sheffield's red-light district now, at just the moment another young woman working the street had been murdered? The image of her sitting on the bus came to me again. Was she on her way to meet someone? She still had her bag with her. What happened to make her lose it the day after? I did not know the answer to any of these questions but it was five days since that bus ride, she may have been in Sheffield all that time, and was perhaps here still; indeed, I could imagine her moving in the streets around the restaurant where I sat eating, and I had the curious sense of her deliberately eluding me, as in a game.

The waiter came to clear my plate and I complimented him on the food and asked if his name was Karim, and he replied that it was, so I explained myself and asked if he would be willing to answer a few questions.

A Sheffielder from birth, Karim spoke in the soft, raw accent of the city. He was thirty-three years old, he told me, and lived with his wife and two children in Hillsborough, near the famous or perhaps notorious football ground, though he'd never been interested in football, a game for stupid people, he said, unlike cricket. His children didn't agree, he added at once, with a sort of smiling sadness. He had a range of smiles, in fact, from shy to brilliant, which he deployed more and more as we talked. He refused to sit with me, preferring to stand, a little awkwardly, by the table, but his modest, perhaps anxious, manner disappeared as our conversation went on and he became almost chatty, as if discovering that he liked being listened to. Yes, he said, he'd worked in the balti house in Upper Allen Street, for some time, nearly three years in fact, but the location wasn't great, tucked out of the way on a dark street with that dirty alley and condemned brick shed next to it. There had been a murder there, he told me in a hushed voice. For a while, sickeningly, more people came to eat at the restaurant because of it, like tourists seeking out a local site of special interest, but in a little while they stopped coming at all and soon afterwards it closed. The best locations were undoubtedly further south, on West Street or, better still, on Devonshire and Division Streets, where so many bars and restaurants were located. He was knowledgeable about the restaurant business and when I enquired about the practice of dumping unwanted produce he immediately confirmed that it went on. It was so costly to dispose of out-of-date uncooked meat according to procedures that a few restaurants sometimes dumped it instead. Worst was when they dumped it in other restaurants' bins. It had happened to them once in Upper Allen Street, he said, a rotten half-pig turned up in one of their bins. Probably, he added, this sort of thing went on more frequently than they realised because the refuse collectors often neglected to check and took the stuff to landfill anyway.

It made sense and of course provided a possible explanation for the extra weight in the balti house's wheelie bin on the morning after Ella had been attacked. I thanked him and paid and he brought hot towels and mints, lingering by the table as I prepared to leave, as if wanting to talk more, so I took the opportunity to ask about the sex workers in St Vincent's. His reaction was visceral – he no longer smiled. He thought the sex trade an abomination, an insult to his religion – though when I asked about individual women, he was more upset than angry, even sympathetic, particularly when talking about the women soliciting on the street who were, he said, desperate people, victims of their addictions, vulnerable to their minders and the worst sort of men who used them. His disgust was reserved for the women in the parlours and saunas, who had the perverted idea of sex as a normal profession. He had known a girl, he went on quietly, who had ended up on the street. A nice girl. She was just not very strong and lacked people to help her. He stared at me in silence for a moment. The last time he saw her was in hospital. She'd been keeping a phone for one of the other girls, a girl from Romania, which was against the rules but the sort of risk the girls took for each other; and the girl's minder had found out. She died, he told me in a flat, apologetic voice, and stood there, breathing.

I showed him a picture of Ella Bailey taken from the footage on the bus. No, he said, he hadn't seen her around, but then he was no longer based near the streets where she might work. I should try Shepherd Street or Kelham Island. He thought the other women there would recognise her.

It was time to go. As I left, he seemed to revert to a more reserved role, saying, almost bashfully, that he hoped he hadn't talked too much, and I reassured him, and he brightened and told me to come back soon, and next time to try the mixed grill.

Back in my Airbnb I found a message from DS Nunkoo telling me that Caine Poynton-Smith had been released on bail; the Crown Prosecution Service wanted more direct evidence of his involvement in Sly Stones's murder. She was disappointed but thought that with a little more time they would build a strong enough case to see him in court. She was certain he was hiding critical information. I thought about my own conversation with him in that interview room, how he had broken down so easily under questioning. I have known people whose collapse into incoherence is, deliberately or not, a means of concealing something. Like Nunkoo, I doubted Caine Poynton-Smith had told us all he knew, and I sat there trying to remember everything he'd said and how he'd behaved, not only in our interview but also at his house in Jordanthorpe the day before. For instance, I remembered his confusion when I asked him if he'd seen Ella recently and I began to wonder what exactly he'd been confused about.

Towards the end of the afternoon my phone rang – an overseas number I didn't recognise. A woman speaking hesitantly with a curious accent told me her name was Olivia Brookmyre and that she'd heard I wanted to speak to her. A Detective Sergeant Nunkoo had contacted her, she said. She'd been a pupil at Whirlowdale School a dozen years before, she added. It was the girl whose father had been sports master when Ella was expelled. I thanked her for calling and explained what I wanted to talk about. She hesitated. She wasn't sure she could help me. She knew next to nothing about Ella, she said. Ella had been a year older; Olivia had never even spoken to her. Her only connection with her was a strange incident which had taken place when they were at school. I said it was that incident I wanted to talk about and after another hesitation she began.

Although she was the daughter of the Head of PE, she herself was never sporty, she said, a source of disappointment to her father, who had been a junior long-distance champion in his own youth. By contrast, Olivia was short-sighted, uncoordinated and timid in competitive situations.

Shy too. Not many friends. One of those mousy girls standing alone at the edge of the playground clutching her satchel to her chest, she said, and laughed, a little uncertainly. Ella was the absolute opposite, she went on, as I no doubt already knew, a legendary figure. Children often take their identity from their attributes, she said, they're given roles, someone is famous for maths, someone else for naughtiness, someone for sex appeal. Well, Ella was the great athlete. I said that, according to her teacher Ms Bell, Ella had very few friends herself, and Olivia was silent, considering that. Ella was different, she said at last, marked out, special, a national champion, and perhaps trapped inside that role by other children who were reluctant for her to be anything else, like a friend. Or perhaps that was her nature, to be alone. In any case, she went on, Ella was always alone on the track, where, almost every night, Olivia saw her while waiting for her father to finish work, never daring to say anything to her or in fact even approach her. She paused again, perhaps remembering the same scenes which had stuck so vividly in Ms Bell's memory too, Ella repeating her routines, a blur in the twilight, her footsteps exploding out of the darkness. She must have had a training programme, she said, which she performed each night with great discipline. But one day, to Olivia's surprise, Ella wasn't on the track. Olivia's father had discovered that she'd stolen some equipment from the school gym. He'd been furious, his trust had been betrayed and, to make it worse, other teachers – Ms Bell was one of them – had accused him of acting irresponsibly in giving Ella unsupervised access to the equipment in the first place. In response, he decided to report the theft to the police and ban Ella from representing the school again. Olivia overheard him talking about it to her mother and, instinctively, felt a sort of horror; not a rational response, of course, rather a childish, superstitious fear of what school would be like if Ella wasn't on the track every night as usual, if she was no longer the great athlete, if her legendary status were obliterated. It would have been like one of the school buildings collapsing, she said. So she argued with her father and, to her surprise, he reconsidered. It should be remembered, she added, that Ella was the most promising student athlete he was ever likely to coach.

She hesitated, as if unsure how to proceed, then went on, in a quieter voice. At the time, she said carefully, things had been difficult for her personally at school. To be blunt, a boy had been bullying her. He was three years older, his bullying was sexual and she was too ashamed to tell any adult, though typically, she added, other children knew more or less what was happening, sensing it intuitively, as children do, and, just as instinctively, for their self-protection, blocking it out. Children are stronger than adults, she added, capable of greater suffering, they have different codes of conduct to which they bind themselves, less rational but, like magic, more powerful. She was telling me this, she said, in order to explain what had happened.

Unknown to Olivia, her father had mentioned to Ella how his daughter had argued for her reprieve. Ella must then have asked around about Olivia and found out about the boy. After that, as I already knew, Ella assaulted him – and the bullying stopped. In retrospect, it seemed a clear case of consequence: Olivia did something for Ella, so Ella did something for Olivia. But at the time, she went on, that wasn't how it appeared at all; on the contrary, what Ella did seemed totally unconnected to what Olivia had done. Olivia wasn't aware that her father had mentioned her to Ella, nor that Ella had asked her classmates about her, nor did she know what had actually happened on the playing field, which was described by everyone as an unprovoked attack. And Ella behaved throughout as if Olivia didn't even exist, even in those last days passing Olivia in the corridor, standing near her in the canteen, without any recognition at all. It was only later, Olivia said, that, bit by bit, she discovered the truth. Finally, someone who had been on the playing field that morning confirmed that Ella had told the boy to stay away from Olivia, and that he, no doubt outraged, and, besides, two years older than her, much bigger and a boy, had naturally struck out at her, not expecting her furious response.

In any case, Olivia said, Ella's behaviour remained inexplicable to her, even now. She still couldn't connect it to herself. So far as she was concerned, the bullying just stopped, not to resume for a long time, nearly two years, and when the boy did attempt to bully her again, she was confident enough to call him out. What Ella had done, even in retrospect, seemed much more a private ritual enacted for reasons of her own, a trial of her principles, or a challenge not unlike the challenges she set herself on the track, something she had to do alone, which she refused to diminish by sharing it with Olivia or explaining it to the teachers who demanded to know the reasons for what she had done.

'But, really, I have no explanation for it,' she said.

I replied that perhaps explanation was off the point and that the important thing was to intuit, like a child; and she said that children may be good at intuition but no good at knowing how to act, which of course was true.

She hesitated. She wasn't going to ask me what had happened to Ella Bailey, she said, she didn't want to know. Over the years, she'd trained herself to remember Ella only as the girl on the track, a fast-moving blur in the twilight, not the other girl she didn't understand. She'd reduced Ella to her childhood role once more, she said, the safest thing for her to do. Children are strange, she said in afterthought. Adults too, of course. The difference is that children know it and accept it.

I sat in my Airbnb, in a chair by the window overlooking the street, watching the light weaken and thinking about the fourteen-year-old Ella Bailey, a fostered child, of an age to be dissatisfied and distrustful, whose remarkable athletics talent set her apart, indeed set her on a different path altogether, a future already beginning of coaches, sponsors, sports journalists and other adults, though she lived still in the world of school, as a child and in the strangeness of childhood. Not thinking strategically but, as Olivia had described it, instinctively, or perhaps, putting it another way, fiercely determined to do the right thing – as her father had taught her. And as I imagined Ella marching across the playing fields to find that boy, I found myself thinking of Anne Elliot in *Persuasion*, another self-denying woman, trained to do the disciplined, self-punishing thing. And this made me think again of Ella sitting on the bus just five days earlier, staring ahead of her, concentrating on her own thoughts. I was more convinced than ever that she'd returned to Sheffield with a definite purpose in mind, and I did not like it.

I left the Airbnb and walked towards the red-light district, but I did not get there. As I passed the café on the corner of Edward Street, I happened to notice who was sitting there and changed my plan.

If Puck was surprised to see me at that time – a little after ten o'clock – she didn't show it; she seemed preoccupied, in fact, sitting alone at the window with an empty cup. She barely looked up as I sat down next to her, and I asked her if anything was wrong. Her father was forcing her to leave her apartment, she said at once. As I'd anticipated, he'd caught up with the news about the recent murder and, without consulting her, had cancelled her lease and paid an early-departure fee. I bought her another coffee and she began to brighten; she was young, of course, and also self-aware. What her father had done was to demonstrate once again the failures of patriarchy, she said, but she would refuse the opportunity he'd given her to theorise, she wouldn't allow him to find refuge in the general male failure, for he was a particular and specific arsehole, she said. Of course, she went on, not all fathers are bad, and without warning asked me if I had children. After a moment I said that my son had been killed in a car accident, obviously a difficult thing for people to hear, especially when unexpected, causing all sorts of awkwardness or distress and more often than not evasions of various sorts, from the well-meaning to the self-protecting, but Puck at once stood and put her arms around me, a spontaneous and natural act expressive of her unguarded self.

We sat for a while in the reverberations of that moment not saying anything, then she asked me if I'd found my sex worker yet. I said not yet, no, but I had a new photograph to show her and she looked at the image of Ella from the bus CCTV footage a long time, with interest. The beret's all wrong, she said at last. It doesn't match and it looks lopsided. That was interesting. But she didn't recognise Ella and hadn't seen her working in the streets around the café. I remembered that Puck liked to talk to sex workers and I asked if she'd picked up any information from them about a new woman on the streets. Now she looked embarrassed. She'd never managed to actually talk to a sex worker, she confessed. They knew she was a student and were suspicious of her. Perhaps they had in mind the rumours that female students were offering amateur sexual services on internet sites to supplement their student loans, undercutting their market, or perhaps the women just disliked students, with their money and daddies and comfortable futures, winners in a world in which they were the losers, or, then again, perhaps they simply didn't want anything to do with her. Which was fair enough, she went on, particularly because, she added with a faint blush, her original intention had been to involve some of them in her dissertation project, with footage shot on the streets and voice-overs, but they had closed ranks against her; not surprising, because they were such a tight unit, and she could see now how her proposition might be considered exploitative. But anyway, she said, I could try down by the rail station, which is where she'd heard new girls began, not necessarily because the older girls drove them out of the red-light district, though that probably happened too, but because in any group there's such a thing as seniority.

I thanked her and finished my coffee. Perhaps, I said to her as I prepared to leave, your father cares about you after all, and she shrugged and gave a crooked smile, and then I left her there in the window with Andreas Georgoulas standing behind her, totally ignoring her, as I imagined he ignored everyone.

★

Night staff at a rail station are not always easy to find but I eventually found one returning from the car park, where, he told me, he'd been seeing off a group of kids selling drugs. 'Schoolkids,' he said. 'If you're not shocked, you should be.' I said I was shocked, and we talked as we walked alongside the arches of the stone facade, lit up now with old-gold light thrown up by lamps set into the ground. It was a quiet, placid night. Across the plaza ahead of us was a long shining ribbon of steel and water commemorating Sheffield's heritage, and, further up the hill, the tower blocks of Hallam University, all hard-edged black geometry against the pale summer night sky. His name was Dennis, he told me, and he'd worked late shifts for nearly four years and it had cost him his marriage. Just look at me, he said. He had a jittery manner, rubbing his slack unshaven cheeks and plucking at his tightly curled grey hair while he talked. Yes, he said in answer to my question, the hookers came down from the centre, sometimes they showed themselves here, he said, meaning the plaza, but generally they loitered in the car park along the side, where it was dark. Handy for the punters, he added. He wasn't surprised anymore, just saddened. When I showed him the picture on my phone, he made a performance of his response, putting on his glasses, taking them off again, holding the phone close to his face, turning it this way and that, enlarging the image and shrinking it again. Yes, he said at last, he'd seen her. He sounded surprisingly definite. Was he sure? Absolutely sure. When? 'Just last night,' he said.

I looked at him carefully but he didn't waver. This sort of time, he said, midnight maybe. Not in the plaza, back in the car park. The beret stuck in his mind. Bright pink, he said. And the birthmark. Besides, he said, surprising me further, he'd talked to her.

I asked him to tell me about it.

They hadn't talked long. She was a hooker, he added in case I hadn't picked that up. He was just finishing his rounds and she stepped out of the shadows, like they do, and asked him if he'd got a light, and he told her he didn't smoke, and she said neither did she, and laughed. He'd told her she couldn't stop there but she ignored him.

I asked him what she'd been wearing, and he said the usual stuff, short skirt, stockings. That beret. And how did she behave? He gave that serious thought, rubbing his tight dry curls with his fingers. It was odd, he said, because he'd encountered dozens of hookers over the years and they all had the same manner, they fixate on you, he said, they don't want to let you escape, but this one was different, after that initial exchange she seemed indifferent to him as a potential punter. She'd asked him if he'd been on his shift long, and he told her a couple of hours, and she asked him if it had been busy. Just chit-chat really.

I asked him if he could remember any more of this chit-chat and he made an effort, wincing slightly.

She told him she was looking for someone, he said at last.

Who?

'Her dealer,' Dennis said. She hadn't said that outright but it was obvious from the way she described him. White guy, she'd said, dark hair, twenties, wearing a baggy jacket. She didn't mention his name, of course. She wondered if Dennis had noticed him waiting for business in the car park, selling stuff out of a bag. Dennis rolled his eyes and shook his head at me. Hookers, dealers, he said. That's what you get on nights. It had worn him down. Personally, he hated the dealers, for a long time he used to call the police every time he saw one, though it didn't do much good, he said, they always came back again. Anyway, he told her he hadn't seen any dealers for a while and before she could come on to him again with her pitch, he put an end to the conversation, told her she had to move on, didn't she realise all this was property of Network Rail? And then, Dennis said, he returned to the concourse and when he next went back to the car park it was empty.

End of story, he said.

I asked Dennis about the bag.

'What bag?'

Did she say what sort of bag the dealer had?

'Nothing special about the bag,' Dennis said. 'Ordinary. Red kitbag, she said.'

I thanked him and gave him my card and asked him to call me if he should by chance see again the young woman or, in fact, the man with a red kit bag; and then I went back to my Airbnb.

As I walked down the hall I could hear music coming from Puck's apartment, the same sort as before, dreamy and ambient, more like a soundtrack to a movie than a playlist of tunes, but as I drew closer it came to an abrupt end, as if she'd heard me outside her door and was waiting for me to go into my own apartment before continuing. I remembered what she'd told me the previous day about seeing a man with a red kitbag. Caine had unconvincingly denied having such a bag but he was unconvincing in general and I did not want to read too much into his response.

I went into my apartment and sat with my laptop and began at once to run CCTV footage from the railway station to which DS Nunkoo had already given me access. I didn't think I should waste any time. As before, I had the sense that Ella was eluding me, as if she guessed that now she'd returned to Sheffield there would be people looking for her. But why had she returned, what mission was she on? Was the man with the red kitbag really her dealer? I thought again of that fourteen-year-old schoolgirl marching across the playing field to do something which would have nothing but bad consequences for herself, and was afraid.

There were cameras outside the station covering part of the plaza and cameras on the footbridge over the tracks, and on the furthest two platforms. There were no cameras in the car park. I knew it was going to be a long night and I made myself a thermos of coffee and began to review the footage.

Towards morning I found her. Not touting for business, not meeting the man with the red kitbag, but boarding the last train to Chesterfield just a few hours earlier. In fact, at exactly the time I'd been standing in the plaza at the front of the station talking to Dennis she'd been on Platform 7; we'd missed each other by a matter of minutes. So it turned out that she'd gone to the station for the most obvious reason of all: to catch a train. It had taken me a moment to recognise her, though. She wasn't wearing her beret or the tinted glasses, her face looked naked without them and something had happened to her hair. Her physical manner was different too, no longer self-possessed but hesitant. There was a moment when she'd almost reached the edge of the platform when she turned sharply to look behind her, as if frightened she was being followed.

Chesterfield station is a small affair with that traditional wooden canopy roof the English like so much, and, outside the entrance, a bronze statue of George Stephenson, 'father of the railways', a solemn, balding man with beetling brows holding up a tiny model of his first locomotive train, a father indeed, sternly offering his child a toy if only they will be good. Across the car park was the famous crooked church spire, sharp and twisted like a big bent tack, and to my right the taxi rank. As usual, the drivers were a tight-knit group, used to being together, knowing each other's routines and good at remembering their fares, and I was soon directed to Omar from Kazakhstan who recognised the young woman he'd driven the night before. She looked just like she did in the bus CCTV still I showed him except for the fact she hadn't been wearing a beret. Omar had seen that her hair didn't grow on one side of her head, where there was a lot of old scar tissue. He remembered that. I asked him where he'd taken her and he told me a late-night Londis on the Chatsworth Road, and I asked him to take me there too.

Fran in Londis looked a long time at my police affiliation but only a short time at the photograph of Ella, whom she recognised straight away. Yes, she said, she came into the store quite often, usually in the evening, to pick up a pint of milk or half a dozen eggs. No, she didn't know her name, though she did know the name of her daughter who often accompanied her: Maddy. That was interesting. How old was Maddy? Fran shrugged. Thirteen, fourteen? Did Fran know where they lived? No. Obviously somewhere near. Had she ever seen Maddy's father? She thought about that. No, she said at last. Sorry she couldn't help more. I said that on the contrary she'd already been a great help, and she could help me further by pointing me towards the nearest secondary school. As I left, she called after me: they'd never had any trouble with her, she wanted to make that clear. I thanked her and would have said that she wasn't in any trouble now but I wasn't sure about that.

★

Chesterfield is mainly a low-rise town of red brick, and Chatsworth Road is a long line of terraced housing punctuated by cafés, barbers and small shops selling things like wedding dresses and carpets. After half a mile or so, I left the main road and walked through more red brick, older at first, then less old, until I came to a new housing estate and just beyond that, set apart in its own grassy grounds, the Manor Hall School.

The school was rightly strict about giving out information and it took a phone call from DS Nunkoo to persuade them to let any of their teachers talk to me, though in fact all I really needed to know, Maddy's surname – Clarke, it turned out – the receptionist let slip during my first conversation with her. While waiting for Nunkoo to provide me with an address, however, I took the opportunity to talk to Maddy's form tutor.

Mr Williams met me in his office, though he was usually to be found on the playing fields or in the gym, he said. He was one of the sports masters, a stocky young man from the South Wales valleys with short fair hair and a habit of flexing his arms as he sat, as if trapped, behind his desk. He appeared distracted and didn't immediately grasp who I was and what I wanted. Maddy was in lessons, he said; besides, I would need formal permission to speak to her. At last he understood. Yes, of course, he said, he knew

Maddy's mother, or stepmother, he should say. Tessa. Great lady. Challenging, he added, which was not a problem, he was a challenging person himself, he liked a person who spoke their mind, even when they had wrong ideas, as she did. He laughed to himself. It seemed she'd made complaints about the provision of athletics at the school. She was an individualist, he said, she didn't really get teams, didn't understand the ethics which underpin sports at all schools now. He himself put the focus on girls' rugby, though it was a battle trying to involve Maddy, who wanted only to do dance, which maybe wasn't the best thing, because frankly, he said, her body shape was all wrong – though he had no problem with different body shapes, he added. Apparently she was good at dance. I asked his opinion of Maddy as her form tutor, and his interest in her dropped a little. A good kid, he said. Yes, happy enough. You always know if something's wrong at home, he added. Not particularly academic. Normal kid, no big issues. He trailed away.

Nunkoo called me with Maddy Clarke's address and I thanked Rhys for his time. Before I left, I asked when he'd last seen Tessa. Not for a while, he said. She must have been away. Usually, he said, she came to school to meet Maddy every day, not because she had to – Maddy was fourteen, after all – but he got the impression they were very close. If you wait here you might catch her at the school gates, he said. I thanked him again but said I wanted to speak to her straight away. He called after me. 'Tell her I'm going to get Maddy into rugby if it kills me.'

Meadow Rise wasn't far away; it was quicker to walk than wait for a taxi. I was very close to Ella now. Soon I was hurrying through a quiet estate of detached houses with smart forecourts and neat lawns, wondering what journey had brought her here. Although I never rehearse what I'm going to say to people, I began to imagine the moment of meeting her at last.

The door was answered by a man wearing the white overalls and dusty boots of a painter-decorator. His name was Rob, he said. He seemed to be in his thirties, a lean man with a thin face framed by straight fair hair darkened with grease.

'Missing persons?' he said. Before I could answer, he thanked me for coming so quickly and led me into a living room at the back of the house looking out through French windows on to a small paved garden laid out with stone ornaments around a pond in which I caught sight of a silver fin.

He was already beginning to talk but I stopped him.

How did he know who I was?

He looked at me, puzzled. He said he assumed I'd come about his partner.

I said I had. I'd come to talk to her.

He was more puzzled still. 'But I've just reported her missing,' he said.

So it didn't end but began again in confusion. Rob did not want to listen to me, he wanted to tell his own story, which was urgent enough. For a while, I let him talk. He'd reported Tessa missing half an hour earlier after coming home at lunchtime and finding her gone. She'd been away for a week visiting an old friend up in Tadcaster who'd just had a baby, he said, and had only got home the night before, very late. He'd hardly had a chance to talk to her, just briefly at breakfast before he went off to work. They had an arrangement to meet at lunchtime. But when he came home she wasn't here. There was no note. She didn't pick up when he called. He'd called the Star Inn on the Chatsworth Road where she worked in case she'd gone in for a lunch shift, but she wasn't there. He'd called round friends but no one had seen her. He called the hospital but she wasn't there either.

Pushing hair away from his face, he looked at me expectantly.

'How does this work?' he asked. He was full of that bright anxiety almost indistinguishable from eagerness.

I said carefully that before we focused on Tessa's recent movements, it would be helpful if he told me a little bit about her. How long had they lived together? If he was puzzled by my question, nevertheless he answered promptly. A little over four years. He met her in July 2020, just after the end of the first lockdown. Like so many pubs at that time, the Star had adapted, with outdoor booths and all the usual precautions, and he took Maddy there for a meal out and Tessa served them. Strange way to meet, he said. She'd been wearing a mask, of course. For months, in fact, he never saw her whole face, only her eyes. I asked if he knew when Tessa had started working there. Just a week or two before they met, he said. Lucky for the Star, he added, with all the job shortages then. Then I asked him a question which I knew he would find strange. How much did he know about Tessa's life before they met?

He hesitated, beginning to suspect that something was wrong. He became very still, as people sometimes do in moments of fear, and as he spoke he peered intently at me, watching my reactions. Tessa had never talked much about her past, he began. She'd grown up in Sheffield, where she lived with her mother, he knew that. Her father was never around. Then, when she was eighteen, her mother died. Lung cancer. She'd left Sheffield and for a couple of years lived in London working, believe it or not, as a stunt performer in the movies, but on the set of the new *Bad Boys* film she had a serious accident, falling from a crane, and was in hospital for a couple of months. He touched the side of his head. Her hair never grew back, he said. Anyway, after that she decided to move back north and look around for something quieter.

He stopped speaking and looked at me hard as we sat together in the silence. He said, 'You're going to tell me something I don't want to hear, aren't you?'

I said that I was sorry.

Some people would instinctively have fought against it, but he remained calm; perhaps he'd never quite believed what Ella had told him. He went out of the room and I could hear him speaking on his phone to someone in Tadcaster; then he came back and sat down again, letting it sink in, not knowing how to begin, beginning at last, as we often do, at the edge of things. 'Ella' doesn't sound right, he said. She's much more a 'Tessa'.

He pulled himself together, an actual, physical manoeuvre in his chair. 'Listen,' he said. 'All this.' He winced and made a gesture as if to cancel it out. 'I don't care what she's done,' he said. 'Maybe I will. Right now, I want to know she's alright. You understand? I want you to do your job and find her.' So we turned to practicalities: more questions. No, he said, she'd never mentioned to him someone called Michael Godley or Caine Poynton-Smith or Lauren Gissing or anyone else I asked him about. No, she'd never talked about a part of Sheffield called St Vincent's. At my request, he looked for her phone and couldn't find it. No, he couldn't remember anything she'd said or done since coming home that was even slightly unusual, though, as he'd said, he'd hardly seen her.

He wanted to know if I thought she'd got herself into some sort of trouble. She was the sort of person to step forward and sort out a problem, he said, someone who acted instinctively, careless of risk.

There was the sound of a key in a lock, the front door opening, and a few moments later a round-faced girl appeared dressed in the grey Manor Hall School skirt and blue top. She had dark hair in plaits and when she spoke, looking from her father to me, asking what had happened, I saw that she was wearing braces. Rob told her simply that Tessa wasn't at home and he wasn't sure where she was.

Probably, he said, it was simply a misunderstanding. Maddy stayed by the door, thinking about that. 'It must be serious,' she said, 'or he wouldn't be here.'

I got up to go. There were many reasons why someone might temporarily go missing, I said, only some of them serious. Most people return home very quickly. I thought that would happen in this case. Okay, she said, and disappeared, and we heard her going up the stairs. Rob took my details and the details of the community liaison officer and others, and I asked him to call me at once, at any time, if he thought of anything that might be of interest.

On my way out I stopped to look at a framed photograph on a sideboard, a holiday snap showing Rob, Maddy and Ella linked together on a pier somewhere, bright in sunlight. Ella was wearing a baseball cap, those chequered tinted glasses, and dangling gilt earrings in the shape of horseshoes. She was laughing.

'Greece last year,' Rob said. 'She loved it.' His voice trembled as he spoke.

As I left, he was already on his phone, doing what so many immediately begin to do, make contact, ask questions, solicit advice, but also, simply, talk to someone, to feel less alone. As I stepped out of the front door, Maddy silently appeared and stood beside me on the path. 'I don't believe you,' she said. 'He's been crying, and he never cries.' She herself was calm, and it was clear that she was a shrewd girl who would not be satisfied with an adult's evasions, though, as I told her, I was not the right person to talk to her about her mother. So we stood there at an impasse for a moment, and she looked at me with that appraising expression, and I said at last perhaps she could help me. Had she talked to her mother in the morning?

They'd talked at breakfast, before Maddy left for school. Maddy had asked her about her friend's new baby and about her friend and a bit about Tadcaster, but mainly, Maddy said, Tessa wanted to talk to Maddy about her schoolwork, as usual: had she done her History coursework, had she prepared for her Maths test? I asked if she was a strict person. 'Completely,' Maddy said. She was always on at Maddy, what she had to do, homework, exercise, eat healthy, what she mustn't ever do, smoke, take a drink and, especially, do drugs; she was very, very particular about that. I asked if Tessa had said anything at breakfast that Maddy found puzzling or out of character. Maddy thought about that. She's never out of character, she said, that's one of the things about her, she doesn't put on different faces for people like most grown-ups. I asked if she'd seemed glad to be home, and Maddy thought about that for a while. To be honest, she said, she seemed distracted, like her mind was on something else. That was interesting.

Why had Maddy thought that? Her phone, she said. She was constantly looking at it. Checking messages? No, watching something, Maddy didn't know what; a video, girls' voices, giggling, screeching, like it was a party or something. Maddy went into a remembering trance, her face becoming vacant, her voice slowing down.

'We were in the kitchen,' she said, 'and I kept having to repeat everything 'cause she wasn't listening, she was watching this thing on her phone, and I was getting really pissed off, and finally she wasn't listening to me at all, she sort of went blank, just staring at her phone, and it was only when I shouted that she said sorry and put the phone away.'

Maddy began to have trouble speaking. 'I didn't mean to shout at her,' she said at last in a quiet voice. She looked at me. She was a sensible, intelligent girl doing her best. She attempted to say something else and could not. Her face collapsed and she choked out the words 'Please find her! Please!' and before I could react she'd gone back into the house and closed the door and I heard her sobbing behind it.

Omar was no longer on duty at the station but I showed the picture of Ella on the bus to the other drivers and a man called Wilfred told me that he'd picked Ella up near the Londis on Chatsworth Road and brought her to the station early that morning. She'd been going to catch the five-past-nine to Sheffield, he said.

Once again, she'd stayed just ahead of me.

I was tired when I got back to my Airbnb. I hadn't slept for thirty-five hours. I managed to report to DS Nunkoo, and, when I insisted it was urgent, she organised an All Ports Warning. By midday a member of her team had found footage of Ella arriving into Sheffield at 9.30 a.m., exiting the station alone and going across the plaza in the direction of St Vincent's, where two extra patrol vehicles were now deployed. For a while I joined them, walking the streets asking people if they had seen her. Where was she? Why had she rushed back to Sheffield?

At last I could do no more; I went back to my apartment and lay down on the sofa. I couldn't even drag myself into bed. In the few moments before I fell asleep I lay there thinking about Ella Bailey, who had disappeared again, for purposes I didn't yet know. I was very close behind her but still she eluded me. Then I slept, and as I slept I dreamed of her. At first I could only hear the sound of running feet exploding fast and regular in the darkness; then gradually she emerged, running hard, as she used to when she was fourteen, though her face, when it appeared from the shadows, was much older, sunk and scarred as it had been in the police photograph, her eyes weeping, her hair clotted with dirt. No physical deterioration could stop her running, however; in my dream she carried on steadily, not doing her training routines but, it seemed to me, intent on some mission or other, searching someone out across those school playing fields of her childhood, and I could see that she would never give up, and her footsteps beat regularly in my head, solid and insistent, frightening in their furious determination, nagging me until I woke with a start and found my phone ringing with the same furious, insistent beat.

The Medico-Legal Centre in Upperthorpe, which houses the public mortuary, is one of the biggest and most advanced in the country, though it sits modestly enough on unfashionable Watery Street, a long, low brick building resembling nothing so much as a self-storage warehouse. Upperthorpe, like St Vincent's, is all reclaimed land, a mixture of new-build, condemned relics and waste ground, and in fact Watery Street was only half a mile from my Airbnb so I was able to walk there, through the deserted streets and across the dual carriageway, arriving at the centre as the sky turned pale green with dawn light. It was five o'clock.

I was still exhausted, of course, and, in that state, vulnerable to memories, and as I went into the lobby I could not stop myself thinking of the little funeral parlour in

Shrewsbury, where, one morning just a few years earlier, I'd gone to arrange the cremation of my wife and son. I was to meet my mother-in-law there but she'd been delayed by an accident at her home in nearby Much Wenlock, and I found myself alone with the mortician. Misunderstanding what I wanted, she led me at once into a room behind the front office, where I was shocked to find the bodies of my wife and son laid out under sheets on what looked like couches. I was not used to the English way of doing things, and although, of course, I was no stranger to dead bodies, it goes without saying that these bodies were different, so familiar to me in every detail and at the same time now, somehow, shockingly unrecognisable – two cadavers, not a wife and child – and I was helpless in their presence. Of the minutes I actually spent in that room no memory remains except for one moment when I laid my hand on my son's forehead and felt its alien coldness.

At the centre, I was escorted through to the autopsy suite, a clinically chilly room containing half a dozen autopsy tables on their plinths and any number of mobile basins, weighing scales and, of course, trays of instruments, everything in stainless steel as in a large commercial kitchen. The others were already there, the coroner, the pathologist and DS Nunkoo; and a few minutes after I joined them,

Ted and Mary Bailey arrived, dazed and frightened, to identify the body. They stood together holding hands at the head of the table while the sheet was drawn back; and Mary gasped and put a hand up to her mouth, and Ted let out a deep groan. Mary turned away but Ted seemed unable to move, standing there rigidly, moaning, and when his wife put her hand on his arm he shrugged it off and with an inarticulate cry fell forward on to the table, embracing the body of his daughter. He cried out twice – 'My girl! My girl!' – then flung himself away, stumbling across the room, putting his large hands over his ears as if to block out the noise of his own grief, followed by Mary. Though I went towards them, they hurried away and were soon gone, accompanied by the coroner.

The silence was broken at last by the pathologist, who confirmed the manner of death: trauma to the head caused by a blunt instrument, perhaps a hammer, followed by strangulation. The same method that had been used to kill Sly Stones. Ella's knuckles were badly bruised, her knees too, showing how hard she must have fought, but the blow to the back of her head, probably taking her by surprise, would have almost killed her in itself. Nunkoo told me that Ella's body had been found by an insomniac walking their dog in the early hours in Graves Park, one of Sheffield's many green spaces, just north of Jordanthorpe, where

Caine lived. They had already brought him in for further questioning.

We talked for some time about Caine and the man with the red kitbag, if in fact they were two different people, and, after that, about Rob and Maddy in Chesterfield, and when we finished Nunkoo said that all inquiries concerning Ella Bailey were now part of a murder investigation, and she thanked me for my work and told me that my contract was at an end. We argued about it but although she was sympathetic to my personal commitment and understood that any further contributions I might make could be considered not as overlapping but complementary to the main line of investigation, she was clear in her determination to follow procedure. She was a good, honest, straightforward officer and I had no choice but to respect her decision. I asked, however, if I might see Ella's effects before leaving, and she agreed.

In the little room of lockers adjacent to the autopsy suite, I stood for a moment thinking about Rob and, in particular, Maddy, who did not yet know of Tessa's murder and whose grief, though different from Ted and Mary's, was likely to be as intense. I thought too of Rob's comment that Tessa was the kind of woman to always step forward to face a challenge, and also of Maddy's description of Tessa fixated by the video on her phone, just before leaving Chesterfield and hurrying back to Sheffield.

As I thought of these things, I began to shake and worked hard to suppress my anger, or rather redirect it, for, without purpose, it would be nothing but a distraction; and I wanted now, above all, to think clearly.

I laid out Ella's effects on the table provided, each in its little cellophane envelope. Her phone was not among them. That was interesting. No purse either. There was only a bunch of keys, some over-the-counter painkillers, a return rail ticket to Chesterfield, and the bag itself, cheap plastic, clearly a quick replacement for the one that had ended up on the handles of the late-night café on Edward Street. I put on the plastic gloves and examined it. Inside a zippered pocket I found a newspaper cutting from the *Chesterfield Post* reporting a recent youth dance event put on by Manor Hall pupils, featuring a photograph of the troupe, at the back of which was a round-faced girl with dark plaits and braces; and as I stood there with the softened piece of paper in my hand, I reflected on the obvious and crucial question I had failed to answer: why had Ella left behind her comfortable, safe life in Chesterfield, with her new partner and new daughter, to return to St Vincent's at a time of danger? Something had compelled her, and I thought again of that incident at school years earlier when she took on a bigger, aggressive boy in order to pay back a girl who had helped her out. I reflected also on the fact that, five years earlier, Ella had disappeared in March, not to reappear until July, and I thought that if I could find out where she had been for those four months, I might know the answer to my question. All this time, lost in these thoughts, I'd been idly poking about in Ella's bag among the tissues and other bits and pieces at the bottom of it, gazing blankly at them, dreaming almost, and it was to my surprise that at some point I found myself holding up something which at last demanded my attention. In itself, it was not in any way extraordinary. On the contrary, it was very ordinary. An orange sweet wrapper.

But at that moment I understood. And my anger threatened to get the better of me.

I called Nunkoo and discovered that she'd already blocked me. My access codes for all police databases had been invalidated. I went out into the bright morning sunlight and began to walk quickly back to St Vincent's.

By the time I reached the Edward Street flats it was hot but still early and I had to bang on the door for several minutes before Loz finally opened it, scratching her tangled nest of hair, looking terrible and complaining about being disturbed. I told her I had something very serious to say to her and she must have caught my tone because she stopped shouting at once and led me into the room where we'd sat before. She wouldn't look at me, though, squirming on her chair and peering around miserably as she smoked. Her eyes were crusted and red. She'd heard the news.

For a while we sat in uncomfortable silence. Finally I spoke to remind her of something she'd said to me before. 'Best not to tell the police too much.' Sensing what was coming, her agitation increased. I told her that I'd found

151

an orange sweet wrapper in Ella's bag and she looked at me in anguish.

'She was here,' I said. 'Wasn't she?'

She cringed away from me so fearfully that at last I realised the truth. Ella had actually been in the flat while I'd been sitting there talking to Loz just three days earlier.

'In the back room,' she said in a small voice.

I tried to recall what Ella might have overheard. Loz had told me that five years earlier Ella had left Caine and he'd come looking for her with a hammer, that was one thing. More generally, she'd learned that I was reinvestigating her disappearance, and I wondered how this might have made her change her plans. I remembered the odd feeling I'd had earlier of Ella deliberately evading me, and I thought now about her abrupt return from Chesterfield to Sheffield as if she suddenly felt she had to move urgently.

Loz was looking at me nervously for my reaction. I was angry with her, but anger wouldn't help me here, Loz was a fragile mechanism that would cease to function if shaken too firmly; nor, of course, would it bring back Ella; so I told her instead that we were now going to have a proper conversation in which she was going to be truthful, for Ella's sake.

I knew what had happened, I said. Just over a week earlier, immediately after Loz had been attacked in the street, when she was frightened and feeling alone, she'd done what most people would do, reached out to someone she could trust. That person was Ella, whom everyone else thought was dead. And Ella had come, she'd responded at once, didn't think twice, she left her safe life in Chesterfield and returned to St Vincent's to look after her.

Why would she do that?

Loz remained silent, chewing her bottom lip, her eyes darting round the room.

Because, I said, five years ago, after *she* was attacked in Upper Allen Street, Loz had looked after her.

'Yeah, well,' Loz said at last. 'Girls have to stick together.' Frightened at being found out, she became defensive, defiant even. The girls had to look out for each other, she said. Everyone hated them, the police, the punters, their pimps. The fucking students, she added, with their snooty looks and OnlyFans side-hustles. There was no one who would even listen to them, let alone help them. They only had themselves. What else were they to do?

She seemed glad to have got this off her chest and, in fact, having her secret exposed calmed her, as often happens, the anxiety of concealment falling away to be replaced by the desire to tell the whole story. She lit another cigarette. She'd never forget it, she said, that March morning five years earlier. Very early, half past five or something like it. She'd been woken suddenly by banging, not loud banging, weak banging, but insistent, banging like pleading, she said, and when she opened the door, Ella fell through it and lay unconscious on the floor. She was drenched in blood, her head split open, nose shapeless, her neck swollen and twisted, but Loz – as I now remembered – had trained as a nurse and, after the initial shock, forgotten knowledge kicked in. She ran the usual checks and staunched the blood and iced the throat, and it turned out that Ella's wounds were bad but not serious, and in the days that followed, sleeping all the time, she gradually gained strength. Somehow she'd managed to stagger all the way to Loz's from Upper Allen Street without collapsing or attracting attention, which was remarkable, though to be fair, Loz said, the area was often deserted except for the construction guys, and besides, she added, who sees homeless people anymore, or even the sad or the sick, they get tuned out without anyone even thinking about it. There was never any question of involving the police, who would have been more likely to arrest Ella in connection with the armed robbery, nor the hospital, which, like others up and down the country, was already being overrun with Covid patients. Besides, Ella was insistent: from the beginning, she wanted no one to know she was alive; this, she told Loz, was her opportunity to leave her old life behind: she'd already made a start by leaving Caine a few days earlier. Loz knew enough about basic care not to make mistakes in nursing her and though she could do nothing about the scar tissue, which grew lumpy and crooked, Ella recovered. In fact, deprived of drugs, she became healthier than she'd been in years. Of course, she couldn't leave the flat – she spent all her time indoors watching DVDs – but hardly anyone was leaving their home just then, and in general there was a strange unfamiliarity about ordinary life during lockdown which made it easier to conceal a fugitive. So Ella stayed, slowly recovering, until the end of June. Then, Covid restrictions about to ease, she decided to get out of Sheffield. Loz's cousin in Chesterfield offered her a room and shortly afterwards she got a job in the recently reopened Star Inn, which was desperate for staff and asked no awkward questions.

I tried to imagine Ella in Loz's flat those four months. Clever, broken, fiercely determined Ella Bailey. What had she spent her time thinking about? Caine? Her foster-parents? Michael Godley?

I asked Loz if Ella had followed Michael Godley's trial. She had, Loz said, she learned that later, though actually Ella had no memory of the attack herself and had eagerly listened to reports to find out what had happened to her.

She had no way of knowing if Godley was really her assailant but felt no remorse at his sentence; after all, he was guilty of the murders of the two other girls.

Out of interest, I asked about the films she watched.

The new *Bad Boys* film, Loz said at once, rolling her eyes. Over and over until she could practically recite it, start to finish. Beginning to laugh, she choked instead and suddenly couldn't speak and sat staring at me in surprise, her mouth open, her creased face as naked as a child's. I'd seen this happen to many people before. All this time she'd kept herself apart from her unhappiness, as perhaps she often did, but now a moment of laughter had accidentally engaged it and she was filled with her grief. They say that, unlike adults, whose grief begins at once but gradually fades in time, children may seem unaffected for long periods, even at the beginning, but suffer sporadic and intense bouts of grief for the rest of their lives; and I wondered if that would be true for Loz too. I fetched her a glass of water and waited for her to calm herself. The most important part of our conversation was yet to come. I wanted her to tell me what had happened in the last eight days.

As I'd guessed, Ella came to Sheffield the day after she got Loz's call, taking the bus from the station to the hospital, where Dr Hussein must have seen her, in fact, and remembered her as one of the two fellow sex workers who'd visited Loz. I also remembered the footage from the bus, realising, too late, that the northward route of the number 75 went past the Northern General at Firth Park. While Loz was in hospital, Ella stayed in her flat alone until, at last, Loz discharged herself and joined her, only a few hours before I turned up.

I asked when Loz had last seen Ella.

'Two days ago,' she said. 'She went home.'

Had she heard from her?

Only once, yesterday morning. She'd called to ask how Loz was, injury-wise, was she still in pain, did she have to need to go back to hospital for any more painkillers, and Loz had said no, which was just as well because to be honest they probably wouldn't let her in on account of her suing them.

I asked if that was all Ella said.

Just a quick call, Loz said. Checking up on her. She was on a train, on her way back to Sheffield.

'What for?'

'To meet someone, she said.'

'Who?'

'She didn't say.'

'How did she sound?'

'Fine.'

Loz watched me while I thought about that. 'Is that it?' she asked.

I said it wasn't. I wanted her to tell me about her phone. She took out a disposable phone.

'Your old phone,' I said. 'The one you said was stolen.'

She looked at me strangely. It *was* stolen, she said. Unless, she added, remembering that she was supposed to be truthful, she'd lost it, unfortunately she often lost things; but either way, it disappeared while she was in hospital and her best guess was that she'd left it on her bedside table when she went to the toilet and someone had taken it, some visitor or, more likely, one of the staff, a hospital cleaner or porter, they were all chronically underpaid, she said, and likely to be thieving bastards. Had she mentioned that she was suing the hospital? You can't have people stealing your phone while you're lying helpless in bed, she said indignantly.

I said that in a minute I wanted to talk about all that but first I asked her if Ella had shown any interest in the phone and again Loz looked at me strangely. Actually, she had. During the hours she'd spent at Loz's bedside, she'd spent time browsing it, sort of catching up with what Loz had been up to.

And was there a video she was particularly interested in? She almost laughed. I really was like one of those clairvoyants, she said. Yes, a video from the night before her attack, not very interesting, a throwaway sort of thing, and in fact Loz had been going to delete it. She'd filmed it outside the Edward Street café, at about a quarter to midnight, and it showed two other girls, slightly off their heads, larking about in the road. They'd got hold of some fancy-dress costumes somewhere and were parading up and down in them. Funny at the time, Loz said, nothing much afterwards – like, now she came to think of it, so much of what seemed to happen to her – and it was odd Ella liked it, she even forwarded it to her own phone so she could keep watching it. I asked Loz to describe it in more detail: where exactly were the girls, where had Loz been standing, what precisely was in view? Loz made a helpless gesture. How could she remember, she'd hardly watched it herself? Sighing, she tried to concentrate. The girls were running up and down Scotland Street in front of the Edward Street café, she said, she'd been standing on the other side of the road, filming. Behind the girls was the long café window and, to one side, Edward Street running away into darkness.

I asked if anyone had been visible in the café window.

She gave another helpless shrug. I said that it was impor-tant and she thought a moment and shook her head decisively. No.

Was anyone else in view?

She didn't think so. But she hesitated. Actually, she said, there was a guy in Edward Street near the café. She remembered because Ella had pointed him out. She'd seemed quite interested in him.

I asked her who the guy was.

She had no idea.

What was he doing?

Nothing much. It looked like he'd been coming down the street, and, when he caught sight of Loz filming him, he'd stopped, scowling, and stared at her and then even taken a couple of steps towards her. Rude, Loz said. She shrugged again. One of those people who hated to see anyone else having fun, she said. She caught my look. 'What?'

I said that I wanted her to tell me everything she could remember about his appearance. It was important, I said again.

She began to whine. She wasn't good with faces at the best of times, she hadn't really paid attention. White. Dark hair? Maybe not. Some sort of jacket? Shapeless old thing.

Could it have been Caine?

She hesitated. She didn't think so. She squirmed under my gaze. 'I don't know,' she said. 'It was dark, I only glanced at it.'

I paused. Was he carrying anything?

She paused too. Yes, she said after a moment. Yes, that's right.

I knew what she was going to say before she spoke.

A red kitbag, she said.

DS Nunkoo didn't want to receive my calls, didn't want to speak to me at all, but she also didn't want me turning up at Carbrook front desk like an interfering stranger. She was a sensible officer, after all, with an interest in being effective, so she agreed to meet me discreetly off-site.

We sat in the window of the café at the end of Edward Street and I showed her where Loz had been with her camera, and where her two friends in fancy dress had been, and where Red Kitbag Man had been. I knew I wouldn't have to over-explain. I simply told her the date and time of the video, and that the man with the red kitbag had been hurrying down Edward Street from the direction of St George's Park, where, as she knew, Sly Stones had been murdered just a quarter of an hour earlier. DS Nunkoo considered this.

'So perhaps she inadvertently caught on video Sly's murderer leaving the scene.'

I said nothing.

'Who is he?'

I said I didn't know.

'Is it Caine?'

I said I didn't think so.

'Are you sure?'

In truth, I could not be sure. Loz thought it wasn't Caine, I said, though I admitted Loz was not a reliable witness. And it was true, on the other hand, that the student Puck, who'd seen a photograph of Caine earlier, had thought it might be.

Nunkoo pondered this. She pointed out that Caine had been seen dealing in St Vincent's recently with what he called his 'bag of goodies'. She kept her expression neutral and I suspected there was something she wasn't telling me, but she was calm and methodical as usual, talking details, making connections. The day after Sly Stones's murder Loz had been attacked in the street, she said, perhaps it wasn't an attempt on her life but an unsuccessful mugging: Red Kitbag Man, whoever he was, desperately trying to get hold of her phone.

I agreed.

Having failed, Nunkoo said, he remained a danger to Loz.

I agreed again. And Ella, I said, would have thought the same thing.

Clearly, Nunkoo said, because she'd been looking for the man, at the railway station for instance, as I'd mentioned in one of my reports. Perhaps, she went on, she managed to find out where he was and came back to Sheffield to confront him. As she rehearsed these thoughts, she watched my face, as if evaluating my reactions. She had something to tell me, she said at last, not yet public knowledge. Caine's flat had been searched and Ella's pink beret found there.

I saw how this changed things.

The team investigating Sly's murder was already invested in Caine as the perpetrator; inevitably, he was now also being linked with Ella's murder. The DI in charge was driving things that way. Caine's explanation of how the beret came to be at his flat was, of course, a garble which would soon be exposed.

I could see what she was telling me. I objected, nevertheless. Politely, she dismissed my objections. I asked to be reinstated. She very reasonably refused. She was ambitious as well as sensible; her way forward lay with the official investigation, not me. We finished our coffees in silence. As we left the café, however, she turned to me, as if casually, and asked if I would be staying in Sheffield for a few more days, and, catching the deliberate blandness of her tone, I said after a moment that I might well do, and she nodded and without saying more left the café.

In my Airbnb I sat thinking about Ella and Caine. I didn't think Caine was Red Kitbag Man for the simple reason that if Ella had recognised him in Loz's video on the day she arrived in Sheffield, she would not have still been looking for him four days later at the rail station. After all, she knew where he lived. I was sure that, privately, the circumspect DS Nunkoo thought so too. But I did think it likely that Red Kitbag Man was Sly's murderer, videoed by Loz fleeing the scene, who had attacked her later to get hold of her phone. In any case, Ella had begun at once to look for him, a search that would necessarily take her back to the world she'd left behind – understanding that she would learn nothing from the St Vincent sex workers as an outsider (as Puck had found out) but only as one of them, dressing as they did, revisiting the same streets, the rail station and all her other old haunts; and I wondered what strange and difficult emotions this had produced in her, and thought again of her courage.

As I sat there, the news came on the radio, headlining

with Ella's murder – described as the murder of a second sex worker – an unusual case, the reporter said, for she had been 'killed twice', once five years earlier and now again. A woman of 'disappearances', he went on, whose addictions or poor life choices had driven her out of hiding to work the streets again at, tragically, just the time another predator had appeared in the city. The extended report came from three locations – the streets of St Vincent's, where she'd worked; the middle-class neighbourhood of Ecclesall, where she'd grown up; and Chesterfield, where she'd been living under an assumed name – though it was striking that in none of these places could anyone be persuaded to join the reporter in his excitable interest, in particular not Ella's foster-parents nor the man and child she'd been living with, whose undoubted 'agony' the reporter sensitively referenced.

She was dead but I was still searching for her and I still had the sense that she was deliberately eluding me. I switched off the radio and sat in silence, thinking about disappearances. Dr Hussein had told me a few days earlier that they were a normal part of people's lives, and she was right, but of course I myself dealt in abnormal disappearances, by their nature difficult and involving. In my training I was always advised to clarify my thinking about them by suppressing any personal feelings such as disgust or, more distorting still, sympathy; but I've found this impracticable – particularly since the loss of my wife and child – and in fact I've come to think that if emotions sometimes distort analysis, distortion is sometimes exactly what is needed.

Ella had disappeared three times in all. Firstly, five years ago, vanishing from Upper Allen Street. I knew where she'd been and why. Secondly, seven days ago, leaving Chesterfield, pretending that she was visiting an old friend in Tadcaster. Again, I knew where she'd actually been and why. But she'd disappeared a third time, leaving Chesterfield only a day after returning home – it seemed in haste – and going straight back to Sheffield, where she would be killed less than twenty-four hours later. Had she seen something new in Loz's video, which she'd been watching while Maddy tried to talk to her? It seemed very possible. Was the person she told Loz she was going to meet Red Kitbag Man? I thought it likely. But the possible and the likely are not always reliable indicators and I allowed myself instead to think about the girl Ella had been. What came to me, as so often before, was an image of her marching across that playing field in search of the boy abusing the sports master's daughter. I had, of course, already registered her determination, her recklessness, her need to fulfil an obligation, but perhaps I had not sufficiently imagined her feeling for the danger the girl was in.

This too might have propelled her. If Ella had returned so quickly to Sheffield it was because the man she was going to confront was an immediate danger to Loz.

Towards the end of the afternoon, I received a message from DS Nunkoo, sent, I noticed, from a personal account. The message itself was blank but it had an attachment, which I found to contain reports and transcripts of interviews with witnesses and potential suspects carried out in the days after the murder of Sly Stones – altogether, more than a hundred pages of text and images. It was a great professional risk she was taking in sending them to me but I knew why she'd done it and began at once to read.

Several hours passed. As I feared, I found nothing about Red Kitbag Man. Nothing in the statements of the dozen or so sex workers, which were short and anxious, nor in those of the twenty or so men involved with them, which were angry and dismissive; not in that of Caine himself, which was interestingly dishonest but not in the slightest revealing, nor in that of Dean Burton, who wasn't even in the city on the night in question but visiting his mother in Mexborough, who nevertheless managed to provide the longest, most uselessly detailed testimony. In short, there wasn't a single mention of anything that might plausibly suggest even the existence of Red Kitbag Man. So I concluded that the police had missed him completely. Loz's video was the only evidence that he had been on the spot when Sly Stones had been killed. It increased my anxiety. By now it was 9.30 p.m. and there was nothing more I could do by sitting in my Airbnb so I went out in the hope of finding sex workers I might talk to.

I went, first, along Scotland Street, then into the streets to the north, Shepherd Street, Smithfield, Allen Street, and finally over the dual carriageway to Kelham Island, encountering everywhere the familiar sight of graffiti-covered industrial buildings, fenced-off fields of smashed brick and new high-rise for students, streets now dark and deserted at night, where my footsteps echoed with a dead sound. Here and there, I found young women standing in shadows in twos or threes, emerging as I approached with their standard phrases, turning from me quickly to melt back into the shadows. A few agreed to talk. Three of them recognised my description of the man with the red kitbag, though none could tell me much about him and what they said was fuzzy, contradictory. Was he Caine? No one I spoke to knew Caine. They'd seen the man around, that was all, carrying his bag. He was either a punter or a dealer, he had a squint or not, he was from Sheffield or wasn't, he smoked or didn't. He was white, they thought. One of them, who thought he was a punter, said she'd heard he was a choker. Another, who thought he was a dealer, said he had a 'lot of stuff' to sell. Try St George's Park and the student campus zone, she said, where dealers make big sales to students taking a little walk on the wild side. I asked them if they thought he was dangerous and they thought about that for a while and said at last that it was hard to tell, most men act dangerous, it was a thing they all did and a bit of a bore, but most were harmless or if not harmless just unpleasant in the ordinary ways. I thanked them and retraced my steps, heading for my Airbnb. It was 11.30 p.m. But as I passed the Edward Street café, I saw a familiar figure sitting in the window and changed my mind and went inside and ordered an espresso, which Andreas served me without a flicker of recognition.

Dean had varied his outfit a little, wearing a turtle-neck sweater instead of his shirt and sleeveless jumper, which, with his sunglasses, gave him the ridiculous air of a 1960s television personality. But he seemed jumpy. Before I could speak, he told me that he had a 'grievance', which he wanted to share, having been reprimanded at one of his regular parlours that night for taking food into the jacuzzi. Admittedly it was against regulations, but frankly, he said, he didn't see the point of jacuzzis into which it was forbidden to take food; and if the coleslaw had been spilt in a moment of excitement, it was only to be expected and should be accepted by the business as a normal occupational risk. He'd always found food erotic, he added, and coleslaw in particular.

There was no meaningful response I could make to this, but before I could ask my questions, he went on, talking in a more agitated fashion – but as if it were a natural extension of his grievance – saying that he'd heard about the murder of another prostitute. He was clearly rattled. Was it the same man? Had the police made any progress? What on earth was happening to his neighbourhood? His mother, who was not well, was extremely alarmed, he said. I began to lose patience and interrupted him to ask about the man with the red kitbag. Distracted, he was filled at once with the self-importance I remembered from our previous conversation. Yes, certainly, he'd seen him. Yes, a white man in his late twenties or early thirties with dark hair and a certain look, a scowl or even a squint, with a red kitbag slung over his shoulder. Not Caine Poynton-Smith, no. He was emphatic about that and I believed him. Dean knew Caine and didn't like him, a disruptive presence, he said, who had several times upset Dean's ladies. Dean didn't like dealers either, he went on, or girls who used drugs, he'd never once given custom to such a girl. He was in danger of delivering a lecture on the consequences of narcotic addiction and I interrupted again to ask if he was sure Red Kitbag Man was a dealer. He was certain, Dean said. This was his world, he knew the area better than anyone, he knew the people, both the girls and the men, he was a well-known figure himself and, besides, he said modestly, he was observant and intuitive. He'd temporarily lost sight of what I'd asked him but recovered quickly and went on. Yes, the man with the red kitbag was a dealer, he could be certain because he'd actually seen him one night with a customer just outside the café, he'd walked past the two of them and had heard them discussing a deal; perhaps not everyone would have picked up what was going on, but he happened to know the jargon. 'Apache,' he said. It was street slang for some drug or other, he wasn't sure exactly which. Anyway, the 'customer' had asked about this 'Apache' and Red Kitbag Man had replied that it depended on the shifts. 'Maybe Thursday,' he'd said, or perhaps 'Tuesday', Dean couldn't remember, but the point was that he could get hold of some soon and return to make the sale. This was more, much more, than I'd expected from Dean, and I thanked him, finished my espresso and left him there looking very much the man of the world, pathetic and self-deceiving perhaps, but, in this instance at least, undeniably helpful. For 'Apache' was slang for fentanyl, and now I knew where I might find Red Kitbag Man.

When she appeared in the little white room where I was waiting, Dr Hussein told me that she'd thought a lot since our last conversation about missing people. It seemed to her, she said, that many are missing 'to themselves', as if they'd lost their true selves and searched now to recover them. She thought in fact that this search for a lost self frequently underlay what people did, particularly as they got older. In her own case, she said, she found herself increasingly keen to speak Arabic to her children and to cook Iraqi dishes for them, not simply to recreate a little of the culture in which she'd grown up or to pass it on to a new generation, but to find again a sense of who she used to be, the person she'd left behind when she came to the UK, a self she feared would otherwise be lost. It was precisely because she felt she was no longer this person that she clung so fiercely, but probably vainly, to this idea of constancy, she said.

It was an interesting idea. As she led me to her office, I thought of Ella Bailey. Superficially, she seemed to fit Dr Hussein's model, having dramatically left her childhood self behind and become someone utterly changed in adult life, a change vividly captured in those two photographs of her, first as a joyful teenager winning a race, second as a police suspect broken in health. But, in fact, her most obvious characteristic, it seemed to me, was precisely constancy, repeating in later life what she'd done as a child, recklessly acting to fulfil an obligation, adhering to a code of conduct first instilled in her by her father when she was a child. And in this constancy, once again, she reminded me of Anne Elliot in *Persuasion*.

When she was settled at her desk, Dr Hussein asked me if I'd found the missing person I'd been looking for and I replied that I had, but that sometimes both losing and finding can be ambiguous, because unfortunately I'd found her too late.

She was silent a moment, then asked me why I'd returned to see her. I'd talked to the other young woman who had been in hospital, I said. Lauren Gissing. 'The trouble-maker,' Dr Hussein said. Yes, the complaint Lauren had made relating to the loss of her phone while in hospital and what was referred to as 'negligence and disrespectful behaviour' was already wasting her time. In that case, I replied, I had good news. I'd spoken to Lauren and she'd agreed to drop her complaint.

She clasped her hands together. '*Ya'tik al-'afiya!* You don't know how much time you've saved me.' She gave me a shrewd look. 'Is there something you would like me to do for you in return?'

'*Shukran.*' I thanked her. There was something, in fact, and I explained, choosing my words carefully. There was now an investigation into the murder of the young woman I'd mentioned and, as part of that, it was likely there would be a formal inquiry about thefts of prescription drugs from the hospitals in Sheffield. It would take time, however, so I wondered if she'd heard anything about thefts which she could share with me informally. She said that it wasn't hard to grant my request; it was no secret that a man working in an adjacent department had just been suspended, suspected of such thefts, and she understood that the matter was already being referred to the police. The man's name was Stephen Platt, she said, and he was a lead operating department practitioner – assistant to one of the anaesthetists. Over a period of a couple of months, a large number of ampoules of fentanyl to which he had access had gone missing or had been broken, emptied of the drug and filled with water. Security around drugs in the hospital was so tight, she said, that he was always going to be quickly caught; he must have been desperate or reckless to attempt the thefts. But by all accounts, she said, he was a menacing person, disliked and feared by those who had to work closely with him. She herself felt a sense of unease when encountering him even briefly in her department. Recently, in fact, he had appeared for no reason she could understand, though now it seemed likely he'd been trying to access the department's medications unit.

I asked if that had been while Lauren was in her care.

It must have been at that time, Dr Hussein said. Yes. Though as far as she knew there had been no contact between them.

I asked if there was a picture of Stephen Platt on the hospital staff website and she hesitated only a moment before calling it up on her desktop screen. 'There,' she said. 'I don't expect to see him here again. I suppose he's spending his time at home, wherever that is.'

He stared out at us from her screen, a white man in his thirties quite like Caine in looks but thicker set, pale and unshaven with bristly dark hair and thick eyebrows. He did not seem to have a squint but there was a sort of slippage about his eyes that gave him a scowl both impassive and unstable.

I thanked Dr Hussein, we exchanged the customary farewell expressions, and I went out into the corridors, where I immediately called DS Nunkoo.

I kept calling her throughout the afternoon but she neither answered nor called back, and in the end all I could do was to leave a message for her which explained what I had discovered, together with Stephen Platt's name and address, which a police friend in Sevenoaks had obtained for me, and, after that, prepare to go out.

I've never minded surveillance work, though of course it can be tiring, if done well. Traditionally, the private investigator sits in a car or perhaps nurses a coffee in the window of a café, but I was glad to be outdoors. It was a pleasant evening. Woodseats was a quiet district in the south of the city. The shops on the main road had something for everyone, a little Italian trattoria and a large KFC, nail bars and up-scale fashion boutiques. The houses on Cobnar Road, curving gracefully uphill towards a skyline of trees, looked neat and well-kept. At the bottom were those red-brick terraces typical of Sheffield rising step by step; in the middle were pebble-dashed detached houses set above street level; further up were bungalows; and, right at the top, where the road ran out of street lamps and terminated in woodland, thick now with darkness, was a solitary villa, old and tall and shabby. This was where Stephen Platt lived. The trees which loomed over it bordered Graves Park, and Platt's house stood opposite the footpath leading through them to the park itself, where, a day earlier, Ella Bailey's body had been found, only a hundred or so metres away, in bushes bordering a whippet track. Stephen Platt was not at home, but I knew from his closest neighbour that he was out each evening, generally returning home between midnight and one, so I found a place to wait among the trees and settled in. I continued to check my phone but DS Nunkoo still didn't respond to my messages.

It was a warm night and, at the top of Cobnar Road, quiet. No one came down the path through the woods. Platt's house was a black silhouette on the other side of the road. It was an odd house for him to live in, I thought, too big for one person, too expensive for an anaesthetist's assistant, and run-down, damaged in various places, as I'd seen when I looked round earlier. I wondered if perhaps he'd inherited it and, unable to keep it up, was letting it fall into disrepair. I blamed myself for being slow to find him. When, days earlier, Loz had made the claim that a member of staff at the hospital had stolen her phone I should have taken her seriously instead of dismissing it as fantasy; I should have wondered where a dealer with a 'lot of stuff'

179

to sell might be getting his supplies. Ella had discovered Platt's identity more quickly than I did, even calling Loz from the train to check she didn't have to return to the Northern General to get more painkillers and run the risk of encountering him before Ella had time to confront him. Somehow – from one of the sex workers? – I felt sure she'd found out where he lived.

As I stood there, listening to the night hush, I tried to imagine what had happened forty-eight hours earlier, when Ella was killed. There would have been the same hush, I thought, the same warm air, smells of vegetation, the occasional noise of a bird and Platt's house opposite smothered in darkness. Had Ella come here to confront him? Had she even stood where I was standing now, listening to the same small noises in the trees, waiting for him to arrive? She'd been looking for him, I knew, in public places, down by the rail station, no doubt elsewhere in St Vincent's. A woman of courage and instinct, often headstrong. Headstrong enough to visit him alone at his house late at night? I reflected that the streets may not have seemed any safer to someone who had been attacked on Upper Allen Street – with Sly Stones killed in St George's Park and her friend Loz attacked in Solly Street in the middle of the afternoon. And she'd been moving fast, with little time to reflect, not least because she knew that as she searched for Platt I was searching for her. Perhaps also she thought that Platt would turn out not to be Loz's attacker, and, like the other young women on the street, that his menace was mainly for show. But I knew more than her: from my friend in Sevenoaks I'd learned that a few years earlier, in Wolverhampton, Platt had faced enquiries into a possible violent assault on a woman he'd taken back to his house.

I heard his footsteps before I saw him appear around the curve of the road, climbing steadily. He was wearing a shapeless jacket and baggy trousers with extra pockets, moving heavily and shuffling slightly as he came. He did not carry a kitbag, red or otherwise. It was twelve thirty. He went up the short driveway to his house without seeing me and let himself in, closing the door behind him quietly; and I waited a minute and then crossed the road and knocked.

He must have been surprised but didn't show it. His face was unmoving, and I could see that what had appeared to many as a scowl or even a squint was in fact a sort of heavy-lidded solidity. He had a cut above his left eye and what looked like a scratch mark round his neck.

I said that I'd come to talk to him about Ella Bailey. He asked me who I was and I told him, and he continued to look at me without reacting, then simply turned and went down his unlit hall, and I followed him, noting how quiet

181

his heavy movements were. The room he took me into was out of date by more than fifty years, a small square sitting room at the back of the house. It had a brown tiled fireplace against the chimney breast with an embroidered screen in front of it, two thickset armchairs with lace antimacassars, standard lamps on wooden stands and, against one wall, an old piano with yellowed keys and a book of sheet music faded almost to invisibility curling on the stand. It was an old woman's room, everything in it tattered and soiled. Platt turned on one of the lamps, which gave out a tenuous glow, but left the others unlit. He said nothing, only glancing at me once to make sure I'd followed him. As soon as he sat in one of the armchairs he became very still.

I remembered Loz telling me how silent her attacker had remained as he beat her. I did not want to be intimidated by this silence, so, ignoring it, I looked around the room. It was cluttered with things which looked as if they were never used, ornaments thick with dust, an old-fashioned radio set with a bent aerial, a pile of knitting, and other items unrecognisable in the deep shadows. I did not see the red kitbag.

I asked him if he'd inherited the house from his mother and he said nothing, though he kept his eyes fixed on me. I asked him if he knew what had happened to Ella and after a moment he said simply that he'd heard the reports on the radio. His voice was low and sluggish. I said that I believed Ella had visited him the night before.

He looked at me with a sort of sleepy interest. He wanted to know why she would have done that.

To confront him, I said. To find out if he'd attacked her friend, Loz.

'Loz.' He repeated the name without expression. He did not ask who she was. Why would he have attacked this Loz, he wanted to know.

I said it was because she'd filmed him coming down Edward Street from St George's Park a quarter of an hour after Sly Stones had been murdered there.

He considered that in the same careful manner as before, without speaking or moving, his thickset face completely inexpressive, looking at me as if quietly trying to ascertain what I knew and what I did not yet know, evaluating what sort of a threat I might be.

Of course, I went on, it was likely that he'd taken the opportunity to steal Loz's phone while she was in hospital but Ella couldn't be sure of that and would have feared he might attack Loz a second time to get hold of it.

After a moment he said simply that he wasn't authorised to go into the ward that Loz had been in.

Dr Hussein had seen him there, I said.

He was silent again.

I asked him what had happened to his face.

His expression didn't change. 'Nothing much,' he said at last.

I told him that Ella had a copy of Loz's video. Probably she told him this herself, perhaps threatened to take it to the police. She never shied away from confrontation, I said, and if she came here, I went on, he would have found her difficult to deal with.

He thought about that. Yes, he admitted. He knew her type.

What type is that?

'Talkative,' he said after a moment. 'Bit of a wildcat,' he added with a faint hint of a smile.

So she was here?

He didn't answer, and again we sat again in silence while he watched my face. I thought he had nearly made up his mind about me.

At last he asked me what I thought might have happened at his house last night.

I said that if it was true, that he'd attacked Loz, that he'd killed Sly Stones, he would have been frightened by what Ella was telling him. Forensics information is so precise these days, there is nearly always evidence to be found, on a body, on clothing, in a room. I looked round. Few criminals survive a thorough investigation, I said. He would have wanted, at all costs, to avoid such a thing; and in that case, I said finally, it would be no surprise if, out of fear, he'd killed Ella and dumped her body at the edge of the woods on the other side of the road.

Despite these blunt accusations, he remained silent and contemplative throughout.

After a while, I asked him what he was going to do now.

He hadn't decided yet, he said, and another silence descended and we sat there looking at each other. When he finally spoke again it was to ask where I came from.

I told him, repeating that I was a finder employed to find out what had happened to Ella Bailey and that was why I was here. For the first time he allowed his eyes to leave my face. I heard him breathe. He'd decided that I was no threat at all.

It was obvious I wasn't there professionally, he told me calmly. If I had a line to the police I would have arrived mob-handed, not to mention at a different time of day. If I was doing private work, I wouldn't have come at all: a private guy always lets the police do the tough visits. It must be personal, he said and looked at me with interest.

Perhaps it was, I said. He nodded, watching my face, and after a moment faintly smiled again.

Perhaps what I'd told him was true, he said in his thick, soft voice. Perhaps Ella had come to his house. Perhaps she had an idea he'd done something wrong. Perhaps she even showed him her video, as I'd suggested. But it would have been a risk, he said. Didn't I think so?

I said nothing. It was my turn to remain quiet.

Perhaps, he went on after a moment, she came to offer him a deal. Something simple. If he promised to stay away from Loz, she would promise not to go to the police with the video. It's possible she thought that would keep her safe, he said.

He raised an eyebrow but I remained quiet.

But suppose he hadn't liked the deal? Suppose he happened to know that Ella Bailey would never go to the police because she was wanted for an old crime?

I said nothing. I wanted him to continue with his story.

He smiled again. He was enjoying the game.

Let's say I was right, he said. Where did I think he would do it? Here – he glanced round – in the sitting room? Upstairs in one of the bedrooms?

He lifted his eyes towards the ceiling. He wanted me to imagine it.

There was a basement too, he said, nodding towards the door to the hall.

Still I didn't speak. I wanted to let him goad me.

Then what, he asked. Carry her body through the woods? He thought about that. How much did I think she weighed?

186

She was little, he said, no more than five-six, five-seven, but he reckoned she would weigh heavy. She had that sort of build. Did I really think he'd be able to carry her all the way through the trees into the park?

This too he wanted me to see. He raised his eyebrows but again I didn't reply.

Well, he went on in the same slow conversational voice, perhaps he would have managed it. He was pretty strong. But it would have been dark, difficult to see, easy to trip and drop the body. Of course, there would have been no one around at two or three o'clock, the time he might have been doing it, so if he made a noise it wasn't likely anyone would hear. And there were places, he said, where he could rest. A bench, for instance, where he could have put her down for a while.

He was quiet, as if contemplating the picture he'd created.

I spoke at last to ask him how he knew how tall she was but he didn't reply. Instead, without warning or explanation, he got up out of his chair and, after inspecting me for a moment, left the room. I heard his ponderous steps going down the hall and then, as if the darkness had obliterated him, there was silence in the house.

Dr Hussein had been right, he was a menacing person, but careless too, as criminals often are, too secure in themselves, easily infatuated by the secret knowledge of what they've done, and liable to confess, not directly but in little ways, a gesture, a comment; a game in which to make fun of the nosy parker. Was he fantasising or remembering? Had Ella been here, had he killed her? I went to the door and looked down the hall and up the stairs. Everything in the house was dark. It was silent, and I wondered if he might be hidden somewhere watching me. Then, somewhere in the darkness, I heard a lavatory flush. Stepping back inside the room and looking round it again, I caught sight of his red kitbag lying in shadow to the side of the chair where I'd been sitting and went over to look at it more closely. As I did, I glimpsed something else poking out from under the back of the chair, something narrow and shiny with a chequered pattern – the wing of a pair of tinted glasses, which I recognised at once – and I took two steps forwards and nudged it all the way under the chair with the toe of my shoe; and when I turned I found Platt standing in the doorway, watching me in silence. I could not be sure if he'd seen what I'd done.

I told him I was leaving and he stood there looking at me, as if wondering what to do. Although he'd dismissed me as a threat, he may have been regretting his playfulness. After so long listening to him, I felt my anger surge in me; there was a part of me that hoped he might confront me, but as I walked towards him, he finally decided that I was irrelevant and stepped out of my way.

Didn't I want him to show me the basement, he asked.

I went past him and down the hall. He did not come with me. At the front door I looked back and he was still standing in the doorway of the living room, watching me. I went out and closed the door behind me and walked away down the hill without looking back.

By the time I reached the bottom of Cobnar Road I'd called DS Nunkoo twice more but, unsurprisingly at one thirty in the morning, there was no response; so, when I reached the main road, I called an Uber and, luckily, there was one nearby, and soon I was going through darkened streets across the city. I did not know what Platt was going to do now. Nor did he, I thought. He was careful but also arrogant and I hoped he might feel he had a few days in which to consider his move. For myself, I wanted to move quickly. There would be little point going to a police station where I knew no one and the usual procedures were necessarily slow, particularly because I now lacked official affiliation, so I'd taken the precaution earlier of asking my friend in Sevenoaks not only for Platt's private address but also for Nunkoo's.

At night, the city felt close to the countryside, hilly

suburban streets overlooking nearby woods and fields as we drove west through Millhouses across the river into Ecclesall, up Knowle Lane, where Ella's foster-parents lived, and ten minutes later reached Muskoka Avenue, a quiet cul-de-sac ending in a close-knit semi-circle of modest detached houses in pale brick, each with its front lawn and garage, dim now under street lights and very quiet.

It was necessary to break the quiet, of course, but once the initial alarm was over and Nunkoo had answered my knocks, she quickly recovered her self-possession. In her dressing gown she was, in fact, as methodical and focused as she was in her uniform, and if she felt the awkwardness of the situation she did not show it. She did not ask me how I knew where she lived. When her partner briefly appeared in the kitchen holding a small child, she reassured him at once and he left us alone, and she asked me then to explain myself. I was fortunate that she was by nature a listener; she gave me time to describe Stephen Platt and my recent encounter with him. As before, she grasped the implications at once; she could see that Platt was a much better fit for Red Kitbag Man than Caine, whom, as I'd sensed, she'd doubted all along. I told her that it was clear from the transcripts she'd sent me that the investigation into Sly Stones's murder had missed Platt completely. And finally I told her that, unless Platt had removed them by now, Ella's tinted glasses were under a chair in his sitting room. It was enough. Ten minutes later we were in her car on the way to Cobnar Road, where a patrol car was due to meet us.

The patrol car was there but Platt wasn't, he'd gone.

He'd taken his red kitbag with him, I noticed, though not the tinted glasses, which Nunkoo located immediately underneath the chair. It was two o'clock, so he'd been gone no more than half an hour. The patrol officers went through the house and garden, ignoring questions from neighbours who'd come out to see what was happening, and Nunkoo stood outside making calls, updating the DI in charge of the operation, mobilising other patrols in the area, organising an All Ports Warning and requesting Forensics. Everything was done calmly and efficiently. While she worked, I sat in her car looking at the data on Platt that was coming through. He was thirty years old, born in Sheffield, though he'd moved to Wolverhampton to study and, later, to work, returning only after his mother had died. He'd been employed at the Northern General for six years; previously he worked for a medical trust in Wolverhampton, from which he'd resigned after allegations of sexual harassment. As I already knew, he'd been charged twice with violent assault; now I saw that, in addition, he'd been questioned several times about the abduction of a young woman working as a sex worker. He seemed always to have been single, living alone in rented flats until moving into the house in Cobnar Road, which in fact had been his grandmother's.

Forensics arrived, consulted with Nunkoo and filed into the house with their kit.

I thought of Sheffield lying around me, a big city, dark now, and Platt somewhere in it, a man passing alone under street lamps with his kitbag. He had no car or any other means of transport, as I'd ascertained when I looked round before he arrived home, nor, so far as I knew, anyone to support him. I could imagine him moving slowly through the darkness, an anonymous figure seeking anonymity. He seemed to me one of those people who think their true selves hidden behind their impassivity, that they can pass unnoticed and unknown among others when, in fact, all the time everyone immediately notices their air of menace and marks them out, as Dr Hussein had marked him out in the hospital. Such people can act carelessly or even rashly, feeling clever in their assumed invisibility, wrongly believing that, because their true selves are deeply hidden, their actions will never be discovered. According to the victims of his assaults in Wolverhampton, his violence had been completely unexpected, as if he had suddenly lost control of himself; I could imagine a similar loss of control in his encounters with Sly and Loz and Ella.

Nunkoo joined me in the car. Forensics had found something else, she told me: a gilt earring in the shape of a horseshoe wedged down the side of the chair in the sitting room. I said that Ella had been wearing such earrings in a photograph which Rob had showed me in Chesterfield, and she nodded. For the first time she began to show her emotion, imagining perhaps, as I did, the scene in that dimly lit room, with Ella sitting in the chair I'd sat in, telling Platt what she knew about him, while he listened to her in silence, making the occasional sluggish comment, deciding what to do.

I told Nunkoo that I couldn't imagine Platt getting very far; as I understood him, he was a loner without support and though resourceful, prepared to take risks if he needed to, he wasn't, in my opinion, capable of strategic thinking. He was more ordinary than he thought and would fail in ordinary ways. Nunkoo, who, of course, knew the city much better than me, was sceptical.

Unexpectedly, I received a call. By now it was three o'clock, and I didn't recognise the number. The voice I recognised straight away, however: it was Dennis the night guard from the railway station, and I put the call on speaker.

193

He asked me if I remembered the guy we talked about, the one the girl was looking for.

I said I did.

She'd said he had a red kitbag?

I said that was right.

White guy, twenties, dark hair, sort of nothing jacket?

Yes, I said.

Well then, Dennis said. I reckon he's sitting on a bench on Platform 7, waiting for the 04.58 to London St Pancras.

So it ended, in an ordinary way, with a quiet arrest made at a deserted rail station.

Next day there was no sign of the weather breaking, it continued hot and bright, and I slept late before going out to the café on Edward Street for my breakfast. Andreas was listening to the news report on the radio announcing the arrest of a man on suspicion of the murders of both Sly Stones and Ella Bailey, though he showed no sign of interest in it and of course ignored me as usual. My train home was booked for the following morning so I went out into the streets for a final day in Sheffield, revisiting one last time the blind alley in Upper Allen Street and St George's Park.

In the park, students were strolling past the bushes where Sly's body had been found, chatting by the street sign where her bag had been hung; these places had become ordinary again and I was glad of it. By a bin, I encountered Flynn the vagrant, and he touched his shaggy hair to me as if tipping his hat. 'Hey, Walt.' I gave him some money and he laughed and pointed at a nearby bench. That's where she sat, he told me, and laughed again, and we stood there together looking at it.

I was at a loose end. As if I could turn myself into a tourist simply by walking, I went on to look round the cathedral and the theatre district and on further to the Peace Gardens, where I had a coffee and watched the small children playing in the splash park. It grew even hotter. Nunkoo called to say goodbye and thank me for my involvement. She gave me a quick update. Forensics had found yet more evidence of Ella's presence in Platt's house: fibres from his sitting-room carpet on the clothing she'd been wearing; also, more ominously for Platt, traces of blood. In addition, they had testimony from a sex worker that he'd previously sold fentanyl to Sly Stones. Platt, of course, was saying nothing. It was a shame that they didn't have the video, which I'd described to her, but Nunkoo thought that things were entering their endgame, the commonest ending of police investigations: that's to say the long tail of continuing work, for weeks, months, before, finally, the case is tried and the guilty person convicted.

She also had news about Caine Poynton-Smith. In a new

interview, he'd admitted that on the night Ella first arrived back in Sheffield, she'd got in touch with him and he'd met her in St Vincent's, where they drove around for half an hour or so arguing bitterly. She accused him of attacking Loz the day before, which he denied; the argument ended in a fight and he threw her out on to the street. Shortly afterwards he noticed that she'd left her bag in the car. Some instinct of self-preservation stopped him simply flinging it out of the window, and he stopped at the side of the road and frantically wiped it clean of fingerprints before dropping it into the gutter. This happened on Scotland Street, Nunkoo said, outside the Edward Street café. It could easily be imagined that someone finding it in the road the following morning had hung it on the café door handles, the way people do, to be reclaimed if the owner returned looking for it. Sometimes, she said, the most innocent explanation is the correct one. I asked if Caine had said anything about the beret. He had. In the scuffle in the car, she'd also lost her beret, which Caine found down the side of the car seat a couple of days later and took into his flat, he said, 'for sentimental reasons', not having kept anything of hers before. This seemed strange but also believable. Now that he was no longer the main suspect, his attitude towards Ella had changed, as if he might now begin to think of their relationship as a tragic love affair, that they'd been outlaws together in a world intent on destroying them. In her beret, perhaps, he hoped to find a trace of her presence, something left behind for him to grow maudlin over.

I walked slowly back in the direction of my Airbnb. In the street outside the building, I encountered Puck loading boxes into a Range Rover with a man in his fifties, to whom she introduced me with a conspicuous lack of enthusiasm as her father. While he went back to get more boxes, we talked, and, as once before, she noticed my copy of *Persuasion* and asked if I'd finished it yet. Not quite, I said.

'Spoiler alert,' she said. 'It's got a happy ending.' She looked morosely at the half-packed car. 'Happy endings are such bullshit.' She looked at me sympathetically. 'I guess you know all about that,' she said.

I replied that sometimes finding someone in time to save them isn't possible and looking for them has to be its own reward. Sometimes, I added, in the process it's possible to find something you weren't looking for. Perhaps, I said, it would turn out that her time in St Vincent's had been valuable for reasons that hadn't occurred to her yet.

'I guess,' she said. She was a natural sceptic and enjoyed her scepticism, I could tell. 'Then again,' she said, 'finding is one thing, understanding what you've found is another.' This was also true, and she was pleased to have said it. Her father was coming out laden with boxes. 'He's pissed off with me,' she said. 'Somehow he found my OnlyFans site. Though I don't suppose he understood it,' she said. She looked around her. Her memories of the place were strong, she said. She was leaving nothing of herself in St Vincent's but there would always be a bit of St Vincent's in her. And then she leaned forward and kissed me demurely on the cheek, and I said goodbye and so we parted, she going back into the building one last time and me continuing along the street, heading towards the Tandoori Pavilion, where I'd decided to have my lunch and finish my book. On the way I passed the Edward Street flats and ran into Loz looking as dishevelled as ever and in fact distraught. She looked at me warily, as if I were an agent of bad luck. She had news, she said. Her flat had been burgled. Not burgled, trashed. She wouldn't be able to tell for months if anything had actually been taken, she said, because the whole place had been kicked to pieces, things broken in every room. She didn't think she'd ever see Mascara again, she added.

This was the sort of person she was, she said. Things like this happened to her.

I asked if anyone had seen or heard anything.

No, it had happened late at night when she'd been out and there was music being played loud in a nearby flat so nobody could hear anything, or if they did, they thought it was the party. She'd been calling the police all morning without getting anywhere and now she was going to the local station on the corner of Brocco Street to report it and also to file an official complaint. Her life, she said, was just one shitty thing after another.

I watched her disappear down the street, a waif-like figure, hugging herself as she went, one of those people who seem always to be losing, and losing badly, but are never quite beaten, somehow remaining defiant, surviving, spikily, against the odds. And, as I stood there watching her and thinking these things, a sudden fear took hold of me. It was so shocking that for several minutes I stood paralysed on the pavement. Then I called Nunkoo.

It went through to voicemail and I could only leave a message, so I said simply but as forcefully as I could that Lauren Gissing was now at risk and needed immediate protection.

The story wasn't over, it was all still going on. The ransacking of Loz's flat did not sound to me like a burglary, it sounded like someone still desperately looking for her phone. In my mind, things began to change in relation to each other.

An image came to me: Ella boarding the late train home to Chesterfield. In the video footage, she'd looked unsettled, worried – and now I remembered something else: she hadn't been wearing her tinted glasses.

I stood there.

Ella had certainly been to Platt's house, her glasses had been found there. But had I got the night wrong? Was it possible she'd confronted Platt the night *before* her murder – and had left his house alive?

I stood unmoving on the pavement, people walking round me, and after a moment I took out my phone and made a call. Dr Hussein answered and without bothering with the usual formalities I asked her if she could check whether Stephen Platt had been at work on the day Lauren Gissing was attacked. Perhaps she sensed my urgency because she replied at once that, as she clearly remembered, he'd been an unwelcome presence in her department all day. I thanked her and rang off and stood there on the pavement, trying to think.

Platt was not Loz's attacker. And Ella had left his house alive. Why would she do that? Because, whatever else had happened that night at his house, and no doubt it was unsettling – perhaps in fact he'd assaulted her, I could imagine a scuffle, her glasses coming off, sliding under the chair – he'd told her that he'd been at work the day Loz was attacked, which was true, and she'd believed him and had returned home to Chesterfield.

And then?

Then, the next morning, she suddenly set off back to Sheffield.

Why?

Because she'd seen something new in Loz's video.

But what?

I didn't know, and I continued to stand there, people muttering as they went round me on the narrow pavement. It seemed to me that, from the moment she arrived in Sheffield and went to visit Loz in hospital, Ella had understood what needed to be done and had asked the right questions and worked through answers false and true until she arrived, finally, after many twists and turns, at the truth. Somehow I had to follow her there. And as I stood there without an idea what to do, an image of her came to me, a young woman not just determined and headstrong, indeed often foolhardy, but smart too; and at that moment something occurred to me and I was filled with hope, and I began to walk quickly towards Scotland Street, where I would find a taxi.

We went slowly through heavy traffic, down the long, busy road out to Ecclesall and up the hill, past parks and churches, the sky opening up, all the way to Knowle Lane with its trees and verges and middle-class hush.

I was not welcome at Ella's foster-parents'. They regarded me with nervousness for I had brought them nothing so far but pain. Mary, apologetic, withdrew into silence and Ted glowered as they waited for me to explain myself. They were at first bewildered, then affronted, when I wanted to talk, not about Ella, but about their recent burglary. They'd reported it at the time, they said, the police had told them there was nothing they could do. I assured them it was important for me to know what had happened. In the same angry and exasperated manner as once before, Ted told me that the break-in was undoubtedly the work of some addict, some junkie, rifling through houses to find things to steal in order to fund his addiction. There had been several break-ins in the area at the time, some of them so chaotic and destructive they could only be the work of someone half out of their minds; and, in fact, as he'd heard, the police had their suspicions as to the culprit, a dissolute young man he'd sometimes himself seen slouching around the streets. I asked if their own burglary had shown signs of the same chaotic manner. No, actually, Mary said. They'd only realised what had happened when they found the back door open. There was no mess. I asked if anything had been stolen. The point, Ted said, was not whether anything was stolen but the deliberate trespass and the feeling that they were now vulnerable, that at any time, perhaps when they were upstairs in bed, some youth out of his mind might break in and run amok. No, Mary said, they didn't seem to have taken anything, though there were cupboard doors and drawers left open, so it was clear someone had been going through them looking for something.

I thought about that. I said that, if I remembered, their allotment had been vandalised at the same time. The allotment, Ted said, was where he'd seen the junkie once, it was no surprise that damage had been done there. Somehow they'd got into the shed, Mary said, though nothing had been taken. In fact, they couldn't really say it had been vandalised, it was just that some of the things inside had clearly been moved around. They were looking for somewhere out of the way to inject themselves, Ted said. I asked if the allotment was nearby. Round the corner, Mary said. I asked if they would take me there.

It took them some time to find the key, it wasn't in the drawer where it should have been, but they had a spare, and soon we walked out together. The allotments stood at the back of the library at the bottom of Knowle Lane, a scruffy plot overhung at one side by enormous trees and bordered on the other by a cul-de-sac of suburban houses, a quiet enclave secluded from the nearby main road. An out-of-the-way place to shoot up, as Ted had said.

Or to hide something, I thought.

The Baileys' allotment, no tidier than the rest, was in a spot near the middle. They hadn't found time to work on it in the last few weeks, Mary said regretfully. Ted opened the shed and I went inside. This was his domain, crowded but orderly, shelves full of tins and containers, balls of twine, sprays, packets of seeds, tools racked against the walls alongside watering cans and buckets, a rough wooden table with an old portable hob on it. It had the smell of sheds, sweet like mould, acrid like engine oil. I asked Ted what was up on the top shelf and he said he wasn't sure, that was the place for things he didn't use much anymore, so I began my search there, and almost immediately found what I was looking for at the bottom of an old washing-up bowl underneath a pile of old gardening gloves and ruined paintbrushes. I took it outside and unwrapped it and we all stood looking at it.

'That's odd,' Mary said. 'We've never had a phone like that.'

Back in St Vincent's I called first at the Brocco Street police station, but Loz had already left so I went on quickly to her flat and found her there, still distraught among the wreckage, angry too, because of the offhand manner with which the police had received her complaint. From other

205

comments she made as we picked our way through the ruins of her bookcase and other debris, it was clear that she blamed me for persuading her to drop her other complaint against the hospital. But she stopped talking as soon as I showed her the phone. She looked at me suspiciously. Was she to understand that the police had stolen it all along? I didn't answer that. I handed her the charger which I'd bought on my way back from Knowle Lane and asked her to plug it in and unlock it, and we sat together on her listing couch watching it come to life. It was a fact, I told her, that in a court of law, video evidence is not admissible if it is a copy – only in its original form, on the phone actually used to record it – something Ella had discovered for herself in the aborted trial into her alleged armed robbery of the corner store in Ecclesall five years earlier. It had been important for her to keep Loz's phone safe.

Loz stared at me. Was I saying that Ella stole her phone? When she visited her in hospital, I said.

And what had she done with it?

Hidden it, I said, where it wouldn't be found.

Then I asked her to show me the video, and she got it up and handed me the phone, and finally I watched it.

Night in Scotland Street, a scene of urban lamplight and shadows. Across the road, the window of the Edward Street café, empty as Loz had correctly remembered. Into view come two young women, prancing down the road, one wearing a policeman's fancy-dress hat and pink feather boa, the other, improbably, the top half of a Dalmatian dog costume with its enormous blunt head tilted back on her shoulders and black plastic trousers trimmed with military-looking stripes. As they prance, they scream with laughter and the camera shakes as it follows them to and fro; then the end of Edward Street comes into view, the bottom of the hill, dark in the shadow of the long block of new student accommodation behind the café, and another figure is visible on the corner, a man with a red kitbag over his shoulder, light from the café window illuminating his face. Stephen Platt, street dealer of fentanyl. As he notices Loz apparently filming him, he produces a scowl and takes two angry strides towards her.

I could understand Ella thinking from this that Platt might be a danger to Loz. But now I believed that once she'd seen Platt at his house, she'd returned to Chesterfield, returned in fact to the video, obsessively replaying it, no longer thinking Platt was Sly's murderer, trying to find something else in it.

I replayed it myself, and again, then a third time, and saw nothing more. And then I did. As the video ends, there is a faint flicker of movement further up Edward Street, a background detail, easy to miss. From under scaffolding, for less than a second, another figure is visible, stumbling into sight, running down the street from the direction of St George's Park, where Sly Stones has just been killed. On first viewing, no more than the blink of a shape before the video ends – but, paused and enlarged, distinct enough for me to see the man quite clearly. A man wearing unseasonal corduroys, sleeveless sweater and signature flat cap.

Dean Burton, the harmless bore.

I asked Loz if she knew where Dean Burton lived. Haughton Road, she said; Dean had a ridiculous habit of trying to persuade the parlour girls to go back there with him.

I asked her where Haughton Road was.

'Next to Graves Park,' she said. 'Why?'

Three days later I sat with DS Nunkoo and Dean Burton and Dean's solicitor in an interview room at Carbrook. By then Dean's tantrums had come to an end. He no longer screamed about police misbehaviour or the mental harm being done to his anxious mother or the miscarriage of justice being perpetrated by a corrupt police force; he'd stopped whining and sulking. He was wearing not his turtleneck sweater and flat cap, nor his sunglasses, but sweatpants and T-shirt. Clearly revealed were his black eye, the cuts at the top of his forehead and weals around his throat. He sat silently, sweating and alert, face twitching, as Nunkoo presented him with evidence gathered since his arrest, moving methodically from point to point in her usual manner. Loz's video had exposed his lie that on the night of Sly's death he'd been in Mexborough visiting his mother. Since then, as Dean himself had feared, Forensics had identified various sorts of microscopic matter on Sly Stones's clothing and body: they matched fibres from his flat cap, sweater and corduroys. He could not explain the injuries to his face. In addition, the search of his house in Haughton Road had revealed traces of Ella Bailey's blood, which he had been unable to get out of his living-room carpet, and also, incompetently hidden in his tool shed, a ratchet socket wrench with blood and one of Sly's hairs still stuck to its rim.

Dean listened to all this in agitation, saying nothing. But when Nunkoo read statements from a number of the young women working in the sex trade, unable to contain himself, he began to make noises, savage little barks and hisses. In a final statement, one of the street workers described how, contrary to what Dean had claimed, he often picked up a girl soliciting on the street, driving them to woodland at Parkwood or Burngreave, where he would indulge in fantasies of menace, though in reality, the statement went on, he was considered a pathetic figure, inspiring not fear but ridicule, and was sometimes openly laughed at. The young woman he pestered most was Sly Stones, but she enraged him by mocking him to his face and telling everyone a story about a 'mishap' he'd suffered one night, soiling himself at the moment of climax. Dean began to scream at us. She was filth, he shouted. They were all filth. Women like that. What they did disgusted him. He'd warned her, he said, meaning Sly, she laughed in his face, he told her what she would make him do, and he'd done it, and it was her fault. He would have said more but officers came into the room then to restrain him and the interview came to an end with Nunkoo laying out the charges to Dean's solicitor as Dean was escorted away.

He'd killed Sly in a rage, springing on her unexpectedly from behind, attacked Loz out of desperate fear that she would realise what was in her video – evidence of him fleeing the scene of the crime – and killed Ella when she turned up at his house to confront him with what she'd worked out. His pathetic appearance was to his advantage, for although everyone was used to his petulance, no one expected him to be capable of such violence and hatred. Ella was strong and determined but he had surprise – and the wrench – on his side.

Still, she exposed him. In the end, the video unlocked it all, as she thought it would, even before she'd seen the vital detail, taking the precaution of stealing it from Loz while she was in hospital and hiding it where no one would ever think of looking, not just an out-of-the-way spot, but a place she'd deliberately turned her back on a decade earlier.

I wondered what had it been like for her, breaking into her foster-parents' house to get the key to the shed, revisiting the allotment where, perhaps, she'd been taken as a child? What memories came to her? Did she find things changed, or perhaps, more likely, discover that things were still the same, the same ornaments on mantelpieces and window-sills, the same tools racked against the shed wall, the same carp showing their silver fins in the tiny pond? Did she find herself changed or encounter the ghost of her young self?

The following day, I finished packing and, with an hour to kill before catching my train, sat on the sofa to finish *Persuasion* at last. And Puck had been right: there was a happy ending. It is, obviously, a story about women: the flighty Musgrove girls, who will rapidly find their own husbands; Mrs Clay angling to catch Anne's father Sir Walter; Anne's foolish younger sister fretting about her marital status, and her imperious older one, unrealistically holding out for a better match; and, of course, Anne herself, the great self-denier, like all the others playing the marriage market strictly according to the rules laid down by the men, in her case not striving for what she wants but, on the contrary, subduing her memories, resisting her feelings, standing aside to let rivals vie for her still-beloved Wentworth. How polite they all were, so correct in their decorum, but as I finished it I was filled with emotion not for Austen's women but for the women of St Vincent's and their raw and necessary solidarity.

I received a message from Nunkoo updating me. Platt had been charged with stealing and selling fentanyl. Dean had produced a statement, an outpouring of self-justification in which, almost as an aside, he admitted to his crimes. In the case of Sly Stones, he'd followed her to St George's Park and attacked her in a rage when she laughed at him. Having just finished a late shift at the garage where he worked, he had with him a bag of tools, including the ratchet socket wrench. In Ella's case, he'd panicked when she arrived at his house. Nunkoo added that the attack on Ella five years earlier in Upper Allen Street was, they felt sure, carried out by Godley, who had left her for dead in the bin. For his part, Dean had now admitted that he couldn't be sure Ella's assailant had been smoking; his earlier insistence on the point was simply another aspect of his instinctive attempts to give himself an air of infallibility. Given that Ella had survived that attack, the murder verdict would be retrospectively removed from Godley's record.

It was time for me to leave, to disappear once more, and soon the cleaners would arrive to make the apartment spotless again, to wipe away all trace of my stay. Puck had told me she was leaving nothing behind, but I was seized by the opposite urge. Perhaps Dr Hussein had touched something in me, a need to be found as well as to find, in some small way to confirm my place in the world, as if to imagine myself returning home one day and finding the presence of a small, dreamy boy in an object left behind in a house in Mansur, Baghdad. So I went into the bedroom and pushed my copy of *Persuasion* under the bed where the cleaners would not notice it; and then I left the apartment, going past Puck's now deserted flat, and out of the building.

ACKNOWLEDGEMENTS

I'm extremely grateful, for the usual reasons, to the usual people, namely riverrun publisher Jon Riley and editor Jasmine Palmer, copy-editor Nick de Somogyi, PR directors Elizabeth Masters and Ana McLaughlin and the rest of the wider team at Quercus. In this book, I also extend special thanks to Sami Cohen and Farah Josephs for help with the Arabic. And, finally, as always, my deepest thanks are to my wife and children.